XMAS DUST

MEL A ROWE

The Following Is Written in Australian English

I consider the ELSIE CREEK SERIES a love
letter to the unique individuals that continue to
shape the Northern Territory into a truly
amazing part of Australia.

My dad would've loved it

ZERO

ope is a mistress of mystery, like the mythical muse is to the artist. Hope, some say, lives on a wing and a prayer. Yet, through the eyes of a child, hope is carried on a set of sturdy wings…

Covered in crayon, Monet's paper boat sent ripples across the water reflecting a monster skyline filled with fluffy white clouds in the shapes of elephants, unicorns, and puppets from her picture books.

On the doorstep, which led to the tiny farmhouse, Monet batted at the flies, frowning as the paper boat kept going past the washing line, leaving her behind.

It floated past the thick mass of flies swirling over the wallaby caught in the fence near Mummy's vegetable garden. They'd been counting down the days to eat those strawberries, hoping to beat the ants.

Now there were no ants. No cows to sing to. There were no more wallabies to chase as they bounded across the plains. No grasses to hide in. No Daddy.

It was if the water had swallowed the world.

Monet flicked a bead of sweat from her brow. She wanted to wallow in the water like the buffalos, but she knew crocodiles lurked beneath the silvery surface. Daddy had warned her that all the water around home belonged to the Billabong Bunyip, who was bigger and scarier than a thousand crocodiles.

Tucking her toes under her dress, she blinked at her reflection. Blue eyes, tangled yellow hair, and sweat mixed with dirt streaked across her face. 'Look, Dolly, we're the same.' She held her precious rag doll next to her. The one Mummy made her ages ago.

Her belly rumbled again. Mummy didn't cook anymore.

A low buzzing in the sky caught her attention. It was the sound of a thousand flies, that grew louder. It came from the gigantic shadow of a straight-winged bird gliding down through the clouds.

Was it real?

It flew overhead.

It was a plane!

'Daddy!' Monet jumped back into the kitchen where Mummy stood at the sink staring out the window. 'Daddy made it.' She tugged on her mother's arm. 'He's here, Mummy, come on.'

Her mother wouldn't move, like her baby brother in his cot.

The front screen door banged shut behind Monet as she ran with her rag doll. Waving her arms in the air, she ignored the stinging stones digging into her bare feet as she dashed across the red dirt to the top of their tiny hill.

The plane was beautiful, white, and sleek. It roared above her so fast; then swooped left and came in to land.

'Daddy. We waited, just like I promised.'

The plane skidded its wheels on the red soil covered with a fine sheen of green. They'd never had grass on their driveway before. The shed's roof shone in the sun, but their tractor inside remained underwater.

The plane stopped and Monet rushed for the opening door. 'Daddy?'

She frowned at the man clambering down the plane's ladder. It was their neighbour. 'Is my daddy with you, Mr Kirby?'

'No.' He crouched before the girl, tipping back his hat.

His wife followed in her beautiful dress and matching shoes. Mrs Kirby was so shiny.

'Where is Tucker?' Mr Kirby asked.

'Daddy went away in his boat...' Monet pointed to the river that hid the road to town that was a whole day's drive away. 'Did you see my Daddy in your plane?'

Mrs Kirby gasped, widening her glossy red lips, her shiny fingernails clutching her pretty necklace. She looked like a model from one of Mummy's magazines.

'That child is a feral fright! And, what is that god-awful smell? Don't you—'

'Beryl, enough,' snapped out Mr Kirby. He then turned to Monet and said in a gentler tone, 'When did your father leave?'

Monet shrugged. 'It was a few sleeps ago. We had power back then, but now our food's got maggots—but I kept the flies away from my brother, I gave him my mosquito net.'

'Jeez…' Mr Kirby stood tall, keeping a gentle hand on Monet's shoulder. 'Tim, get out here. Bring that bottle of soft drink with you.'

'Honey,' said Mrs Kirby, screwing her nose at Monet, 'I don't think our boy should be out here with this—'

Mr Kirby silenced Mrs Kirby with one stare as he spoke to the boy jumping down from the plane. 'Share your drink with Monet and both you kids stay by the plane. Watch those dingoes don't chew the tyres.'

Mr Kirby didn't look back. His boots crunched on the coarse red soil, while he swatted at the flies as he headed for the screen door. Mrs Kirby followed, taking timid steps in her spiky shoes.

'Hey, do you want some? It's lemonade,' Tim asked Monet, holding up an icy cold bottle. He looked a few years older than her—nine or ten. 'We'll sit here—hold on, I'd better get a towel or Mum will get mad at me for getting my good clobber dirty.' Tim scrambled back into the plane.

'Your mummy looks like a lady from the magazine.' Monet stood on tippy toes, reaching for the plane's smooth wing. It was cool to the touch.

'We were going out for lunch.' Tim spread out a towel under the shade of the plane's wing. Leaning back against the tyre, he poured two cups of the fizzy soft drink and they sat cross-legged, staring at a world of water. 'A lot of rain, huh?'

'The water just kept coming—it didn't stop.'

'It's flooded everywhere. Dad reckons it's the twenty-year flood and calls this our inland sea,' he said. 'We drove all our cattle to higher ground, knocking down fences to let the livestock through, so the herd's all good.'

'I've never seen the sea.'

'It's goes on forever. We go to the beach every year when we visit Mum's family.' Tim paused to sip from his drink. 'Where did your dad go?'

'To get help.' She glanced back to the last place she'd seen Daddy waving from his small boat. 'Daddy promised he was coming back.' And she had promised to be a good girl and wait for him.

A scream echoed through the house, sending the flock of galahs screeching from the roof.

The screen door slammed against the house as Mrs Kirby ran outside. Her shoulders lurched as she vomited, holding onto the tree.

Monet screwed her face up, finding it hard to swallow the sickly-sweet lemonade.

Tim jumped to his feet. 'Mum—'

'Stay there,' called out Mr Kirby, approaching with forceful steps. 'You two stay right bloody there and don't you dare move.' He climbed into the plane, sat hard in the pilot's seat and started flicking lots of dials.

Mrs Kirby kept retching at the base of the tree.

'Elsie Creek Police, come in,' said Mr Kirby through the radio's handpiece. 'Come in, Elsie Creek Police...' He waited for a reply, staring hard at the floor. 'Come on, Sarge, it's Jack Kirby. I'm sorry to do this to you today, mate, but please, pick up.'

'Elsie Creek Police, here. Go ahead, Jack,' came the gruff voice from the plane's speakers.

'Sarge, I'm at Tucker's place—' Mr Kirby paused, wiping his lips with the back of his hand. 'We've got a situation. There's a dead baby with the mother um...' He hesitated, inhaling sharply as if in pain.

'What about Tucker?'

'Gone. Tucker was meant to visit us last night, but didn't show. We hadn't heard from him in two days, so I did a flyover. The only one talking is the little girl who looks like she hasn't eaten in a week, and the house is flyblown, mate.'

'They'll never get that stench out of the house, I tell you. She was always loopy, that woman,' grumbled Mrs Kirby, wobbling on her heels as she continuously wiped her hands down her dress. Again, and again. 'I told Tucker not to marry that woman, she's crazy. Absolutely certifiable, is what she is.' Mrs Kirby snatched Tim's lemonade bottle and took a long, deep drink. 'When—how—that baby?' She scowled down at Monet.

'My baby brother just never woke up,' Monet said with a tiny voice, cowering from Mrs Kirby. 'He used to cry.'

'Aw, jeez.' Mr Kirby shook his head, speaking into the radio handpiece, 'What do you want us to do, Sarge?'

'Is Tucker's wife alive?'

'In shock, I reckon.'

'Can you bring the mother and child here to the hospital? I'll organise a search crew for Tucker. Let's get that woman and child safe.'

'Will do, Sarge. Over and out.' Mr Kirby jumped out of the plane. 'Beryl, get the kids sorted into their seats. I'll get Emma.'

'What about my baby brother?'

Mr Kirby again crouched before Monet, meeting her at eye level. 'Does your brother have a name?'

'No. I've been thinking of names while waiting for Daddy.'

'Why on earth didn't Tucker take his family?' Mrs Kirby asked.

'Didn't want to risk them. Emma's way too early.' With a tender palm on Monet's shoulder, he said, 'I'm so sorry, Monet, but your brother didn't make it. He's...'

'Dead.' Monet had heard him say it on the radio.

'I'm so sorry. Right now, we'll get you and your mother some help.'

'What about our luncheon at the Kingston's?' Beryl asked.

Mr Kirby frowned at her over his shoulder. The screen door to the house gave out its familiar creak before slamming shut behind him.

'What's he doing with my mummy?' Monet asked Tim, who brushed down his clean jeans just like his mother did with her dress.

'We're all going to town,' Tim said, folding up their towel.

'Town?' Monet touched her coarse hair, full of knots. You had to plan when visiting town, its where she'd have a big bath with bubbles from the shampoo. Mummy would tie Monet's hair in ribbons to match her good dress and shoes, just like Tim and Mrs Kirby were dressed—proper.

With a fierce scowl, Mrs Kirby stormed towards them. 'All that food preparation and effort wasted, I tell you. I've been so looking forward to lunch at the Kingston's since forever. Now, this...' She blocked the sun, standing over Monet. 'I bet you'll end up as crazy as your mother.'

Monet hugged her dolly, biting her lip. She'd promised to be a good girl, and good girls never spoke back to grown-ups—especially those who said hurtful things about Mummy.

'Oh, no, you are *not* taking that filthy thing in our

plane.' Mrs Kirby snatched the rag doll from Monet's arms and tossed it into the floodwaters.

'No! *Dolly!*' Monet tried to reach for it, but it got caught in the rushing current. She couldn't swim and stopped at the water's edge. Tears blurred her vision, watching her doll float away in the same direction Daddy had disappeared.

The front screen door creaked, then slammed shut as Mr Kirby's boots crunched on the dirt.

Monet whimpered, tasting the salt of her tears. Her dolly, gone. Her daddy, gone. Her brother didn't want to play. And her mother was being carried out in a blanket by Mr Kirby.

Mrs Kirby pinched Monet's arm, dragging her to the plane. 'Let's go, you feral—'

'I can't leave. I've gotta wait for Daddy.' Monet ripped her arm free, ignoring the stinging red welts in the shape of Mrs Kirby's fingers, and ran back to the house. 'We can't leave my brother alone, it's not right. I promised Daddy I'd stay.'

The door slammed shut behind her as she hid inside the house's cooling shade by the Christmas tree where the lights no longer twinkled. Christmas cards were strung in a row nearby. Her drawings of Santa giving her family presents were stuck to their fridge buzzing with flies. Her eyes watered at the stench of rotten food from the powerless fridge, leaching slime onto the kitchen floor.

'Monet, we need to get your mother to the hospital,'

said Mr Kirby, coming back inside. 'She needs you now to hold her hand.'

'What about my brother? I promised Daddy I'd be a good girl and stay and look after…' She dropped her heavy head to her tightening chest. She'd failed.

'I'm sorry, but we can't do anything for your brother,' he said, stroking her hair like her Daddy did. 'The police will come and help him. Right now, I need you to be strong for your mother.' He scooped her up and carried her out the door that banged behind them. 'You've got to be the toughest kid I've ever met. You know that?'

'I am?' She winced in the harsh sunlight, staring back at the dark house.

'Oh yeah, Territory tough. I reckon your dad would be so proud of you right now,' Mr Kirby said, carrying her to the plane. 'You'll sit next to Tim, and keep being that brave girl you are.' He clicked her into her seat belt, then banged the door shut.

In front, Mummy stared dead ahead, not saying anything. Mrs Kirby sat next to her, waving her hand in front of Mummy's face. It was rude, but Mummy didn't even blink.

Grown-ups squawked over the radio about search and rescues and last known sightings. Monet heard her daddy's name, Tucker, mentioned, but didn't understand what they were saying.

'Have you been in a plane before?' Tim asked from the seat beside her.

Monet shook her head, clutching her knees as her bare feet swung miles off the floor.

'It's good, you get to see everything,' Tim said. 'We were going out for Christmas lunch. Dad's looking forward to tomorrow, we'll be watching the Boxing Day cricket match and playing with my new cricket set. Hey, what did Santa give you this morning?'

Monet shrugged. So much was happening. The plane's engine rumbled through her chest. The windmills on the wings spun so fast they became invisible.

'Here, you can have this.' Tim held out a small red aeroplane in the centre of his palm. 'This has a propeller that spins so we can fly and the wheels turn on it too. Merry Christmas.'

'Thank you.' Forced back against her seat as the aeroplane accelerated, she gripped the little toy red plane tight, missing her dolly.

'Hey, it's okay.' Tim grabbed her hand as the plane roared down the rocky driveway.

Monet gripped his hand tighter.

'We'll take you home,' he said with those big, light blue eyes and a warm smile. 'I promise to take care of you.'

Comforted by his hand, she clutched his toy to her chest as the world flew by so fast.

'What did you ask Santa for Christmas?' Tim asked her.

'For my family to be home together,' she whispered, peering out the window, watching her home become a tiny house on an island surrounded by an ocean.

Their island had enough room for a plane to land—but not enough for a sleigh?

'Santa didn't come today,' she said, 'So, I must've been a naughty girl.'

ONE

20 years later...

Monet's steady boot steps competed with the rumbling wheels of her backpack, echoing down the corridor of the Unofficial Elsie Creek Inn. Bright light streamed from Rigsy's room, where her younger cousin was zipping up his duffel bag. 'Am I still right for that lift?'

'Yep,' Rigsy replied, sliding on his sweat-stained Akubra. 'You know, you could fly me back home. Mum would love to have you there.'

'I've got a better offer,' she said with a grin. Monet didn't do Christmas. She didn't want to pretend to like the sucky gifts people gave. Stuff watching relatives being fake-nice before arguing enough to stop talking with each other until next Christmas.

Nope, she was looking forward to her chance to escape the whole Kris Kringle load of crapola. Every year she avoided the whole ho-ho-ho fiasco. Christmas was permanently cancelled from her calendar.

Through the lounge, she stepped over the assorted swags holding snoring men stretched out under the whirling ceiling fans. The pre-dawn shadows stretched beyond the open walls of louvres allowing the cool breeze and scents of rain to filter through.

It was a typical sight for the morning after the last big Christmas hooray in town. Elsie Creek may have gone tinsel-mad, as usual, but there was not one damned Christmas tree or bauble inside the Unofficial Elsie Creek Inn, and that's how she liked it.

In the kitchen of mismatched scrappy furniture, Monet refilled her water coolers. She glanced up at the now-bare spaces on top of her cupboards that used to display snow globes that would catch the sunlight, spreading tiny rainbows around the room. Now they were empty, like this place would be in a few hours.

She missed her old housemate, Lucy. Maybe even her handmade Christmas cupcakes, annoying everyone with her Christmas cheer and Santa music loaded with bells.

Jingle bells, bah-humbug!

Bells should be banned!

'Monet,' said the gravelly baritone behind her. 'You can't leave me without a Christmas cuddle.'

She turned to face the stockman in his unbuttoned shirt. His jeans hugged his hips, the shiny rodeo champion belt buckle highlighting his muscular torso. In the typical boots and signature uniform of the slouchy Akubra, he was sexy with a hell yeah! But she was never touching that cowboy. 'Craig, only after you've showered. Who knows what hay bale or bed you've crawled out of?'

'One day yours.' Craig hugged her anyway.

'Honey,' Monet said, trying to push the cowboy with blonde curls away, 'they've already written our lives on the pub's bathroom wall, let's not add to that chapter.'

'Yeah, it'd ruin a beautiful friendship.' But he still hugged her again.

'You know the rule, I never sleep with my friends,' she said, stepping away from the serial-hugger. Monet might not have many rules, but the few she had, she lived by. 'What's happening with Sandy?'

'I'm taking him to Mum's, after we convince the flying vet to fly us home.'

'Good. Thanks for doing that for me.'

'Only for you.' Craig smiled, giving her a wink as he filled up the kettle.

Rigsy barrelled in with a swag over his shoulder, dumping his duffel bag by the rattly fridge. He dragged his esky from the empty space where the stove used to live and started loading it up with ice. 'I've got beef for Mum, beer for me—'

'What about the Inn?' Craig asked, flicking on the electric kettle and reaching for a mug.

'We never lock the back door, because the Unofficial Elsie Creek Inn never closes.' Monet stuck a large laminated notice on the fridge, and one for each side of the back door. It was the same message as always:

Management is unavailable.
Please help yourself and leave the door unlocked.
Any gold coin donations for power & coffee is
much appreciated.
Any issues, email or radio Monet
(WW WW 1)

Monet put out large tins of coffee, tea, sugar and boxes of UHT milk on the bench to keep the guests happy. As there was no stove, that was as far as her housekeeping went. Guests brought their own linen in the way of a swag, and a towel. Plus, they were all well trained to never enter through the front door, herself included.

'Take care, Craig. Say g'day to your mum for me.' Monet scooped up Rigsy's duffel and her backpack and followed Rigsy, carting his esky and swag out the door.

'Will do,' said Craig, waving with his coffee mug. 'Try to be good, if you can.'

'And ruin my reputation?'

'The Station Hand calls you Little Miss Trouble,'

Rigsy said over his shoulder.

'True. I forgot who I was talking to for a second.' From the back door step, Craig gave his wide sparkly smile as he stirred his coffee and tapped the spoon on the lip of the mug. 'Ring me if you get into the type of trouble you can't handle, and I might even put my beer down for a bit to make the hike out to Rigby Downs. I might even take you out on a date, eh?'

'What?' Rigsy said, 'You pair don't date anyone.'

'What is this strange ritual you call dating?' Monet asked, dragging her backpack down the cracked driveway. 'Is that what you do, when you're not playing couch-surfing cowboy?'

'Hey, I've graduated to a proper bed in my room, thank you very muchly.' Rigsy loaded the gear into the rear tray of his Holden Kingswood ute. It was so old there was more grey undercoat patching the vehicle than maroon paint.

'You know, if you want to keep your room at this fine country Inn permanently, just put a lock on the door.'

'Like you, who's never here?'

Monet shrugged, opening the creaky passenger door.

Through the ute's windscreen, she peered at the massive tree towering overhead, with its leaves all shiny from last night's rain. Its thick limbs stretched over the elevated colonial house. Its sturdy trunk stood as the centrepiece of the patchy back lawn that ran through to the stables where scattered utes and horse floats were parked nearby. All would be gone by mid-morning.

It all made up the unique charm of *The Unofficial Elsie Creek Inn* that was a regular stop for many coming to town. It was meant to be her home—the place she was always leaving behind.

Down the cracked concrete driveway, passing the mighty well-lit pub, they turned onto Main Street.

'Who flicked the switch on this place? I need my sunnies,' Monet mumbled, wincing at the multi-coloured, strobing lights crowding the deserted main street of Elsie Creek. 'I think there's a song about wearing sunglasses at night?'

'That might be a name for a new playlist—*Bloody hell!*' Rigsy slammed his foot on the brakes. 'Cecil, you need a set of flashing lights to warn us of your wide load,' he shouted to the short black water buffalo that was standing in the middle of the road, wearing a slouchy Santa hat and tinsel around his horns.

'I'll get him.' Monet grabbed one of the muesli bars from her bag and approached the buffalo. 'Dude, they freaking elfed you!' An over-fed, walking elf. He didn't compare to the many outback elves, made from red-dirt ant mounds wearing Santa hats like Swedish Tomte statues spotted in various roadside paddocks around town.

Cecil's clip-clopping hoof steps echoed off the deserted street as Monet led him to the safety of the sidewalk. Every store window was flashing its own set of bad 80s disco lights—it was enough to give her a migraine.

She straightened the tinsel around Cecil's wide horns as he chomped loudly on the muesli bar like a stranded spectator waiting for the Christmas street parade to start. 'Lucky you're not a reindeer. You'd be forced to wear this crap all year round and jam up my flying space.'

'So says the grinch,' called out Rigsy over the roof of his car, his wide toothy smile yellowed by the one and only flashing set of pedestrian lights. 'Mrs Sternston won best window display this year. It looks good, huh?' He pointed to the brightest window on the street. It was as if someone had stolen the centre of the sun.

'She had inside help, you know that?'

'Are you saying Mrs Sternston cheated? She's gotta be over eighty, or did Tess and those lush legs of hers sway the judges?' He sighed with a goofy grin, his teeth and the whites of his eyes now a hellish red under the lights.

Monet winced against the brightness of the craft store window that sat next to the post office. Slashes of red and white were everywhere. Big red ribbons, a white tree, stuffed animals and towering candy canes. 'Mrs Sternston pays Kat to do her window display. She used to do the big department store windows in the city as a part-time job,' Monet said, climbing back into the ute.

Rigsy steered them down the main street's clash of brightly coloured lights, reflecting off the wet road. 'How do you know?'

'Kat told me last night.'

'When did you hold a conversation with your singing

partner? In between dancing on the bar? You were crazy last night.'

'What's new.' Everyone called her crazy.

'You were crowd surfing with cowboys as if it was your own personal rock concert.'

Her grin grew. 'I'd forgotten about that. We had a mosh pit in the pub.' *Good times.*

'I'm surprised the publican didn't ban you,' said Rigsy. 'You, Kat and the rest of that softball crew were kamikaze karaoke queens last night. D'ya reckon the publican will make karaoke a permanent fixture?'

'Hope not. Some of those cowboys' yodels set off the cattle dogs in the car park.'

'But what a night.'

'Are you sober enough to be under the limit to drive?'

'Are you right to fly?' Rigsy asked, pulling up at the darkened airfield.

'Always.' She jumped out and grabbed her backpack.

'Call me if you need any help at Rigby Downs.'

'I'll be right. Safe trip, young man, and say hello to those that are worth talking to.'

Monet waved Rigsy off at the town's small airport, then flicked on her portable lamp and smiled wide as she approached her pride and joy. The Cessna C206 single engine Stationair.

'Good morning, Gertrude.' Monet patted her red six-seater plane, gliding her hand along the wing like a rider stroking their beloved horse.

She stored her backpack in the cargo hatch. The image of a straw broom stretched along the plane's underbelly, it's glitter glimmered in the torchlight. She removed the tie-downs from under the wingspans and the chocks from the wheels, then went through her pre-flight checklist under torchlight.

'She's good to go, kid,' hollered Mickey, wiping the sweat from his brow with a grey hand towel that matched the colour of his coveralls and thinning hair. He cruised up in his nifty golf cart, loaded with spotlights, dragging a trailer of boxes and scales.

'Of course she would be, especially after she's been tickled by Mickey the Master of all things Mechanical.' But she still checked it over for peace of mind.

A small white ute pulled up beside them bearing the Australia Post emblem on the doors. 'Morning,' called out Tess, wearing green-and-red-striped stockings and red short shorts, with her post office shirt and a slouchy Santa cap. 'We had some rain last night, huh?'

'It's the wet season, it's meant to rain,' mumbled Mickey.

'Well, that explains why I have a floor full of stockmen at the Inn this morning,' Monet said, grabbing a postal sack from the back of Tess's ute.

'Aren't you a bit tall to be an elf?' Mickey asked, gazing up at Tess, who ran the family post office that was part of the town's very busy craft store.

'Did Tess steal your job?' Monet grinned as she

weighed the postal sack, eyeing Tess. 'You got attacked by your grandmother, huh? We even stopped and perused her store window display while sharing brekkie with Cecil this morning.'

'Bloody pest that beast is,' mumbled Mickey.

'Who, Tess's grandma?'

'What? No, I meant—' Mickey wagged his stubby finger at Monet. 'It's too early for your cock 'n bull sass, kid.'

Monet's grin grew as she loaded the bag into the belly of her own beast. 'You look great, Tess.' The woman had the kind of legs that stopped all conversations in the pub, just so the men could watch her walk by.

'Thank you. Grandma made us all outfits this year. She was hoping to do sugarplum fairies, but there are enough tutus running around town now as it is.'

'All I see is bloomin' toddlers in tutus,' grumbled Mickey, weighing another sack before he passed it to Monet.

'I can get you one, so you don't feel left out?' Monet hid her grin, avoiding Mickey's death-glare deepening the creases around his eyes. She loaded the coarse off-white mail sack into her plane's cargo hold. The fancy term was LMB, locked mail bag, and there was one for every cattle station and outstation Monet was expected to visit today.

Tess grabbed another sack from the back of the ute. 'The radio is predicting a cyclone for Christmas.'

'Karma said so at the pub last night,' said Mickey,

taking the bag from Tess. He weighed it then passed it on to Monet to load into the plane. Monet then made notes on her tablet of the cargo's weight, working out her order of delivery. Their loading procession was like a fine-tuned factory line.

'Karma is a crocodile, they don't speak,' said Tess. 'And he's getting fat, the way you mob of men keep feeding him.'

'But he's happy in his custom-made pen,' said Monet, as she strapped down the cargo net over the freight, closed the hatch and started filling up the next compartment. With the bookings she had in freight, her plane had no room for passengers today. 'Why do these bags smell of Kat's candles?'

'How do you know they're Kat's candles?'

'Because Lucy made me do Kat's candle-making class with her. Which I noticed you weren't at.' Monet grinned at Tess.

'I don't do craft,' scoffed Tess. 'And like you, I don't cook either.'

Monet rolled her eyes. 'Just because the Inn doesn't have a stove, doesn't mean I can't cook. I just never follow the recipes.'

'Story of your life, eh, kid? Always chuckin' away the rule books,' said Mickey, winking at her as he passed her a stack of boxes.

Monet lived by her own rules, and that's all that mattered to her.

'How come there is no stove at the Unofficial Elsie Creek Inn?' Tess asked.

'Some cowboy wanted to cook steaks late after the pub closed one night and forgot to turn it off. Burnt the pan dry, set the stove on fire, and nearly took the whole place with it. It was so old I never bothered to replace it and the guests don't miss it.' Monet certainly didn't miss cleaning it.

'So, is everyone getting candles for Christmas?' Her plane smelled of waxy vanilla, jasmine, and citronella.

'You, no,' said Tess, holding out a small box. 'It's the last box left in town.'

'Yesss!' Monet hugged the box of red and white candy canes. The spearmint hard candy was the only thing she liked about Christmas. 'I'm going to name my next playlist after you, Tess. What do you think about sunglasses?'

'I don't, unless I'm looking for some to hide me from the sun.'

A sweep of lights caught their attention as the police highway pursuit car approached.

'Morning, Marcus,' they chorused to the sergeant.

'Morning. I bring coffee and Christmas cupcakes from Lucy, for the pilot and the stations you're visiting,' said Marcus. His police uniform highlighted his solid muscular build as he slid a cardboard box onto the plane's steps. He side-glanced at Tess with her long legs. 'Aren't you kinda tall to be an elf?'

'She's a vertically enhanced new breed of Elf, Sarge,' said Monet as Mickey chuckled beside her. 'You missed the memo, huh?'

'Tess, when are you going to put my poor constable out of his misery and say yes to dating him?' Marcus asked, grabbing his gear from the highway patrol car. 'He's driving us nuts at the station.'

Monet opened her mouth.

'Don't you add fuel to that fire,' said Marcus, arching an eyebrow at Monet.

'I was actually going to side with you, Marcus,' she said, scrambling up her plane's ladder.

'That'd be a first,' mumbled Mickey, passing her the final box. 'You agreein' with a coppa? Are you crook, kid?'

'I'm fine,' Monet said, tucking the boxes away inside the cabin, she then tightly strapped down all her freight.

Jumping out into the muggy early morning air, her boots barely missed the puddle reflecting the lights from Mickey's nifty buggy. With tablet in hand, sipping her coffee, she completed her fuel and weight calculations from the back of Mickey's modified golf buggy.

'Is your flight plan ready?' Marcus came alongside her and unrolled his map, firing up his tablet.

'I'm emailing it to you now.' Monet pointed to his map and explained, 'I'll be over these stations on the north-west, with ten scheduled stops on my way to babysit Rigby Downs.'

'Oh, how is Tim?' Tess asked. 'I haven't seen him in

ages, not since…'

No one had. 'Tim usually visits his mum's side of the family in Esperance for the summer.'

'How long are you staying at Rigby Downs for?' Marcus asked.

'I'll be back a few days after New Year's, unless Tim wants to extend his holiday and hang on the beach a bit longer. Are you having any time off, Sergeant?'

Marcus scoffed. 'Christmas is my busiest time, breath-testing and setting speed traps. Can you do a flyover on the Sandlots? We've heard little from the guy since his wife left.'

'Sandlot Sandy is on the floor of the Unofficial Elsie Creek Inn as we speak. Cowboy Craig told me this morning he's taking Sandy to his mum's for Christmas. Then, we've got Rigsy, who's booked himself in to give Sandy a hand after New Year, until the musters start.'

'Good, that's everyone on the list accounted for.' Marcus tapped the details into the spreadsheet on his tablet. He then pointed to the map's sub-arterial dirt roads that led to town. 'Can you do a road report on the crossings in this region?'

'Sure. Anything else you want on that shopping list? Want me to fetch you some croissants from Katherine, or do a fish count on the billabongs? I haven't done a pizza delivery in a while, or—'

'Just radio through if there are any issues.' Marcus rolled up his map and craned his neck at the purple skyline, laden with grey clouds. 'Weather's getting crappy, there's a low brewing off the coast. Do me a favour and keep the two-way on at the station.'

'You check-in with me at least once a day, kid,' Mickey said.

'I'll be fine.' Monet tucked her tablet under her arm, then shut and double-checked the hatches were locked for take-off. 'Gertrude and I are looking forward to this holiday.'

'What the hell!' Marcus scowled with his coffee cup frozen halfway to his mouth as the sunrise lessened the shadows over the town.

'Oh, no,' Mickey mumbled, raising his grey eyebrows as he stared in the same direction as Marcus.

'What?' Monet asked from the steps of her plane.

'The roof painter got the police station.' Tess pointed to the far end of the runway where the hospital's helipad stood between the outback town's police and fire station.

There was a red cross on the roof of the hospital. A Dalmatian peeing on a red fire hydrant lived on the fire station's roof. And the cop shop had... 'What is that?' Monet asked.

'It's a strong arm holding back a masked burglar carrying a sack. It reminds me of a retro bad guy comic scene,' explained Tess. 'It's very cliché.'

Mickey snort-laughed. Marcus's scowl deepened. And Tess giggled behind her hand.

'It's the long arm of the law!' Mickey let out a

whopping big belly laugh, wheezing for air.

'Not funny,' said Marcus with a frown.

'They tagged the cop shop.' Monet aimed her camera's phone at the art work that covered the entire roof of the cop shop. The image was too dark and fuzzy for her phone to capture. 'It's not light enough for me to post to my Instagram.'

'How many roofs has that tagger graffitied now?' Tess asked.

'Too many, but I'll find out who it is.' Marcus heaved open his driver's door with his eye on the station's roof. 'Safe flight, Monet. Stay out of trouble, and do a radio-check with Mickey once a day.'

'Not making any promises.' To behave, or make a promise she'd never keep.

'Reckon he'll fingerprint it?' Mickey asked as they watched the cop car race to the station.

Monet shrugged.

'My grandmother loves the snail on the post office roof,' said Tess. 'Molly loves her retro woman in curlers so much she wants to refurbish the hairdressing salon to match it. What's your favourite roof painting, Mickey?'

Mickey used his hand towel to dab at the beads of sweat building between the ruddy white whiskers on his top lip. 'I like the Mad Hatter's tea party over the train station the most. It's really clear from the sky.'

'You must take me up again after the Christmas rush is over,' Tess said to Monet.

'Anytime. You don't need an invitation to come party on my mail-run—you are the Post Mistress.' Monet checked her watch, keen to keep her schedule. She had lots of stops to make as the last freight run before Christmas. 'Mickey, the Inn is yours if you get into a bother with your brother.'

'She'll be right, kid. Billy's got us havin' Christmas tucker at the pub with the publican, this year.'

'Just don't play cards together.'

'We don't play, we cheat.' Mickey chuckled, giving her a salute.

She closed her door and pulled the safety lever on the airlock tight. From the windows she waved at Tess, who tooted as she drove back to town. Mickey rolled off in his nifty golf buggy, towing the trailer back to the hangar.

'Gertrude, it's time to get this party started.' Headphones on. Strapped into the familiar mould of the lamb's-wool seat cover. Monet flicked her fluffy dice with the Chinese good luck charm hanging from her rear-view mirror. It was all part of her routine to finalise her cockpit pre-flights checks. She put her tablet in its cradle, with her flight schedule and music ready to start at the push of a button.

The aviation lights came on, reflecting an eerie glow off the wet tarmac.

She started her engine, watching the propeller spin until it became invisible and that's when Gertrude purred.

Monet settled back into her seat, feeling the red plane's rumble as the adrenalin rose.

'Gertrude, let's fly away and leave all our troubles behind us.' They taxied down to the edge of the freshly swept runway that Mickey fastidiously kept clean from any foreign debris, where the white line disappeared on the edge of the wilderness.

Mickey waved from his office doorway, saving her the hassle of radioing the control tower. Above his office roof stood the telecommunications tower, with its top lights lost in the colours of the sunrise creeping along the outback's horizon.

Monet pulled back on the yoke, doing the delicate dance with the pedals, and the roaring plane powered down the white line. Pushing against the mild g-force, she embraced its power.

Wheels off and Gertrude climbed up and over the outlying scrublands that stretched on forever.

This time of year, Elsie Creek was a lazy loping river, with plenty of run under the bridge. It's exposed soft sandbank was a landing bay for the many fishermen and their boats near the town's busy boat ramp.

A lonely set of car lights raced down the Stuart Highway towards Alice Springs. She guessed it was Rigsy cruising down the grey road with the parallel train tracks running alongside. Both road and rail line disappeared on the curve of the horizon.

She banked left to swing wide around the town of Elsie Creek. At the end of the airstrip was the town's first responders' region nestled next to the small country hospital. To the left of them ran the town's main street, aglow with its gaudy flashing red, green and white lightshow.

The roof of the Elsie Creek Tea House came into view. Nearby Lucy's coffee van shone with its tasteful display of fairy lights that spread over the train station's lawn area, where tradesmen, miners, and cattlemen waited in line for their breakfast and coffee. Nearby was the fire chief's vehicle, facing the small-town park that sat opposite.

Over the road stood the mighty Elsie Creek pub, with its lights that were never switched off. Next door was the enormous tree that overshadowed the Unofficial Elsie Creek Inn.

'See ya when I return,' Monet whispered to the Inn below.

She then flicked on her music, loud, and didn't look back. Her eyes were always kept on the sky ahead. There were a lot of stations to visit before she was wheels down and feet up, to relax these next few weeks in peace and solitude where she would miss Christmas altogether.

She could hardly wait.

TWO

From the pilot's seat, Monet bellowed along with the brassy Elle King's *Ex's & Oh's* as she flew over the top of Rigby Downs. She used to love visiting this station to catch up with Jack Kirby, but most of all, his son Tim.

It'd been a long time since she'd been here.

Never as a guest.

She followed the road from town that ran like a jagged red pencil line, leading to a scattering of sheds and cattle yards, which made up only a part of the sprawling homestead. Horses and cattle roamed in paddocks coated in lush, deep green grass that stretched all the way to the purply haze in the sky. Rivers sparkled like glittery rolls of rope. Dams lay as the centre of hand-drawn child-like flowers, with cattle tracks forming the petals and stems.

She buzzed over the airstrip, searching for hazards among the silvery green scrublands shading the red dirt. Cattle and wallabies loved to wander onto the runway. Today it had been wild donkeys and feral buffalos that caused her to quickly cancel her landings, only to herd them away from her flight path to then try again.

Wheels down, the plane skidded on the slushy gravel, but Monet was ready for it. She knew how to slide her way out of any runway party, flying to outback locations long before she was old enough to get a car licence.

Following the fast-moving monsoonal storms, she'd been landing in sticky clay pans for most of the day. It was like skiing down a snow-covered hill, with mud and clay flicking under the wheels, sticking to the plane's body. It was that or the washed-out, rocky roads complete with water-filled corrugations that made her bones rattle and arms ache as she fought the yoke to keep control.

At the runway's end, she turned the red Cessna back towards the small tin shelter that was the gateway to Rigby Down's station.

Normally there would be some sort of a welcoming party.

Most places she'd flown into, the owners greeted her in their mud-splattered vehicles. They'd done their best to clear their sunburnt airstrips for her, many had even mowed it for the occasion.

Here, there was no ute filled with yapping cattle dogs to meet her. No hearty wave from suntanned kids wearing big smiles. No nod from the cattleman's Akubra, or hugs from the wife and station cooks.

There was no one.

Each landing had filled her cramped cabin with humidity, only this time Monet didn't mind. She was simply relieved to be free from the roller-coasting rodeo ride she'd been on all day due to the stormy turbulence. It would have had the bronco rodeo champion, Cowboy Craig, yahooing over the headsets with his hand waving in the air, counting down for the eight seconds.

A weighty silence replaced the engine and music. After hours of plane noise, it was always a jolt to her system.

'Well, Gertrude, we're here.'

She climbed out of her seat, through the back, now empty except for her luggage and personal freight. Lugging back the lock, she jumped out, her boots landing heavily in the soggy soil.

The humidity hit her like steam churning from a bucket of cold water added to a sauna, causing her pores to open and the sweat to start. Cicadas screeched as the hot breeze shifted the leaves of the smooth-barked salmon gums and other native eucalyptus trees. Heat waves shimmered over the runway and along the red dirt track leading to the farmhouse.

The late afternoon sun pierced through the cloud

cover to bite at her skin as she grabbed her water bottle, searching for any sign of life. There wasn't even a sign to say she'd landed at the right station.

'Welcome to Rigby Downs.'

It'd been a long day that officially didn't stop until she had unpacked her freight and perishables. Some days she wished Gertrude was a helicopter; they were much easier to park and to just drop and stop.

But Monet wouldn't swap Gertrude for anything.

Patting the plane's side like it was a steed, she said, 'I'll be right back to unload and put you to bed, Gertrude.'

She grabbed her backpack and hat, and with her aviator sunglasses shading her eyes, she headed down the dirt track.

Nope, this wasn't some episode of *Farmer Wants A Wife* where the willing women were made to walk to the homestead, when Monet knew the farmer was away. Maybe she could start her own YouTube channel on the many ways to keep entertained while housesitting a station?

Her boot stride was steady; she was used to hiking toward homesteads, mining offices or outstations.

As the golden glow of sunset stretched above the crest in the road, she spotted a shiny new shed roof. 'Impressive.'

Tim must've finished the shed his dad always wanted, or maybe it was a horse jumping arena for the new lady of the manor?

At the edge of the homestead Monet stopped in the shade of an overhanging ghost gum. She dug around in her backpack's front pocket, shoving aside her muesli bar stash for buffalos until she found another food source. She then gave a low whistle and waited.

Seconds later, a barking blue cattle dog came tearing down the dirt driveway kicking up dust.

'Hey, Bandit. Just me, mate.' She tossed the dried meat morsel to the dog who stopped short to sniff warily at the meat, then her.

But then it was like flicking on a light switch when the dog remembered her. His stocky blue body moved with the wild whip of his wagging tail as she ducked from his eager tongue-kisses. The black mask-like colourings around his eyes only highlighted their shine.

'Nice to see you too, Bandit.' She patted his coarse fur, giving him another treat as she inspected her surroundings. The sheds were closed, the cattle yards were barren, and the stables were empty shadows. She heard chooks, a few wild birds, and that was it.

She'd been told there was only the one dog. Even so, she searched, always wary when first approaching any station because there was always a dog on duty—and cattle dogs were the worst for sneaking up behind you.

'Come on, Bandit, escort me to the front door.'

Her canine companion trotted beside her wearing a wide smile.

The grand house stood on a small crest, with its deep

shady verandahs and rows of solar panels glinting in the sunlight.

It used to be a place of sumptuous patio furniture and pots of lush ferns. They would hang among Mrs Kirby's collection of wind chimes that used to tinkle with the breeze. It was the perfect place for Monet to read during her summer stays.

But all of the patio furniture was gone. There were no wind chimes. Only a few pots remained, containing nothing but dirt the colour of ash.

Dust lay so thick over the concrete her boots left tracks beside Bandit's paw prints. The fancy French doors were held open by beer boxes filled with empty cans, dumped in a haphazard pile.

She wasn't expecting the place to be open.

She was meant to be home alone.

Stepping inside, she paused at the sound of someone snoring.

Removing her sunglasses, her eyes adjusted to the dim lounge room light. Over half of the furniture was gone, exposing dusty wooden floor panelling. The fancy furnishings that could almost be classed as antiques were replaced with more beer boxes and empty cans. Taking up the wall, was a wide-screen TV playing test cricket.

On the couch, snoring his head off, was the owner. Timothy Kirby.

And her heart just froze.

Oh hell, no!

THREE

The television switching from the calming monotony of cricket to a blast of rock music woke Tim from his drunken stupor on the couch. 'Oi, I was watching that—' Then he remembered he was supposed to be home alone.

He cracked open an eyelid, and there she was.

Monet.

He scrubbed a hand over his face, forcing himself to wake up or sober up, or something. Was he imagining Monet was here in his house?

'You weren't watching. You were doing what they invented cricket for—to sleep.' She dropped the remote like a rock and it smacked hard into the centre of his bare chest.

'Oi.' He flinched and the remote control fell onto the

pile of empty beer cans, which clattered and clanged all over the floor like a drunken strike in ten-pin bowling.

Monet trapped a runaway can with her boot. 'Have a little party, did we?'

'Are you jealous you weren't invited?'

'As if I'd waste my time on crappy cricket and boozy binge fests thrown by…' Monet screwed her nose up at the place and said, 'the Posh Prince.'

She was his forbidden fruit, with that sexy swagger and husky voice he'd recognise anywhere in a crowd. He tried to swallow, but his tongue stuck to the roof of his parched mouth. Why did the universe continually plant her in his path? It was like a never-ending roll of a dice in not how, not where, but how soon they would meet again.

It was always too bloody soon!

Because the woman with the wicked grin had eyes that cared. Deep soulful eyes that saw straight through him, and he hated how exposed she made him feel.

'Don't say it,' he grumbled at her.

'I've said nothing—yet.'

'I know what you're gonna say.'

'Oh, wow, does the Posh Prince suddenly have the gift to read minds? You'd make a fortune if you got off that couch and pimped yourself out.'

He scowled at her. 'Listen, Claude.' He fought the urge to grin at her narrowed eyes. *Ha*, two could play at the nickname pet-hate game. 'Just don't say you told me so.'

'Come again?' She blinked at him, taking a step back.

'You forewarned me...' Then she'd walked away from his path of self-destruction. Or as Monet called it, his headlong downward spiral to crash into his happiness-killer.

Monet sighed like she was carrying a tonne of pain across her shoulders, shaking that soft, dirty blonde mop of hers. 'I didn't want to be right,' she said with such heavy sorrow. It matched the sadness in her eyes. 'I truly wanted you to find your happily ever after.'

Damn. That cut deep, like he'd gone and disappointed her on purpose.

He didn't need this loaded on top of his heartbreak.

'I'm sorry it didn't work out, but...' She arched her eyebrow at him. '... I did—'

'Yeah, I know.' Monet had been the only one who had warned him about his ex.

There was no gloss or polish to the pocket rocket. What you saw was what you got, set in a neat little package that always walked away. It was part of her personal rule book to never make promises, always *lovin' 'em and leavin' 'em behind.*

He watched her walk away in those tight shorts, dragging her bag behind her. Always on the move, flying in and flying out. 'Where are you going now?'

'I'm going to pick a room.'

'You're what?' He sat up in a rush and his head buzzed.

'I'll take the spare room.' Her voice carried down the

long corridor. 'When do you leave?'

'Oi. I live here.'

'I know that, but you paid me to farm-sit over Christmas, which does not include babysitting the farmer,' she said, coming back down the corridor. 'Hey, where are all of your mother's Chrissie decorations?'

'With Mum.'

'Where is Mommy Dearest?'

'Moved to WA to be near her sisters.'

'And left her sweet little Posh Prince home alone?'

'I'm not home alone now, if you're here tormenting me, am I?'

She flicked her wide grin at him like a shot that made him collapse back onto the couch.

'Oh, honey, as much as I love you and enjoy poking your weak spots, I'm busy watching the clock at the moment. The bonus is I don't have to put away all those crappy decorations. So, where are your ute keys?' Monet walked to the kitchen. 'Stop looking, I found them.' She scooped his keys off the hook by the back door and slid on her aviators.

'Hey, where are you going?' He followed her out, eyeballing that confident swagger of hers that was sexy as hell, only to cringe at the bright daylight from the verandah. *What's the time?*

'I'm going to unload my supplies from the plane,' she said, with his dog, Bandit, bouncing after her.

'You're staying?' *What day was it?*

'That's the plan. So, when are you leaving?'

Oi! She was heading to his ute. Patting his dog. On his station.

Keeping to the shadows of the verandah, in bare feet and jeans, he stood squarely, crossing his arms over his bare chest. 'I'm not going anywhere, except to the beer fridge and the couch. I'm on holiday. When are you leaving?'

'When my contract is over.' His driver's door creaked shut and his ute rumbled into gear. His dog jumped onto the back tray and just like that, she drove away.

Bugger! He'd forgotten to cancel her contract.

FOUR

As the sun rose at Rigby Downs, Monet admired Tim's masculinity, which was a marvel to modern man. He was tall, lean and muscular from years of hard yakka that came with running a cattle station. Every time he moved, her body burned with that spin-tail sensation she only got when flying. It made her want to climb that tree and then some.

Even sleeping, Tim was amazing to watch. The way he was stretched out on the couch, it was sweet and sexy all at the same time.

But Monet never slept with her friends.

Especially the Posh Prince, Timothy Kirby.

She wasn't even in the guy's league.

And last night, he didn't play his usual host either. All he did was flop onto the couch to snore in front of the cricket. That left Monet to unpack and attack the kitchen's mountain of mess before she could even start to make herself anything to eat.

Mrs Kirby would have screeched like a hundred fruit bats at the sight of the place.

Technically Tim was her employer on this trip, yet they'd always been friends. Even when Tim's dad paid her for jobs, they'd never made her feel like an employee.

But Tim wasn't acting like a friend either. He was behaving like Mrs Kirby, who never made Monet feel welcome.

Yet, this morning, it was an absolute delight that there were no Christmas decorations to make her eyes ache. Day one of her job when farm-sitting this place was to pack away boxes of garish, shiny crap.

Rigby Downs at Christmas was like someone had raided Santa's cave and dumped it in the middle of the outback. The clashing dazzle of sparkly decorations looked like they'd been tossed around by a bunch of drunken elves who'd overdosed on eggnog as part of some ho-ho-hurl-athon.

Whenever she'd walked through the house, tinsel and glitter had clung to her clothes like cat fur. She was always brushing off the junk.

It was a mammoth job. The first and worst job she always tried to tackle on day one—to get rid of Santa's stamp on the place. Her next task was the bookwork, then the rest of the time was her own. *Hello, holiday.*

This year, with the place barren of all torturous things called Christmas, she was well ahead of schedule.

Flicking on the kettle, she grabbed the dog biscuits and fed Bandit, who was waiting by the back door. She turned on the radio that sat on the shelf above the house phone, listening for the news before she blasted her music.

Scooping up her tablet from the table, she scrolled for recipes to match the food she'd brought with her, to plan her menu for the next few weeks. The kitchen was almost as big as the unofficial Elsie Creek Inn's kitchen. Except the homestead had so much bench space and a fabulous window view of the surrounding countryside over the shiny double sinks. It had a massive fridge that didn't rattle, and cupboards filled with matching crockery and assorted cooking gadgets to aid the home chef in whipping up some magic. Most of all, it had a big-arsed stove she didn't mind playing with.

Walking into the pantry, she blinked at the barren shelves that looked even sadder in the harsh light of the single bulb.

She'd never seen the place so empty.

'Is his lazy lordship becoming a minimalist too?'

'What?' Tim muttered, stumbling barefoot into the kitchen.

She snagged her lower lip to not drool at the guy walking around in nothing but jeans that hung dangerously low on his hips. 'Oh, you're still here.' *Not good.*

'I live here. Remember? When are you leaving?' He reached into the fridge for the milk carton and skulled it back. He then pulled out a small box. 'What is this junk? Tofu! Tell me you're not a vegetarian and a minimalist these days?'

Aww, he remembered she didn't keep junk. 'I'm—'

'It'd be pretty silly being a vegetarian on a cattle station, don't you think?'

'Was I talking to you?' She snatched the tofu packet out of his hands and tossed it back into the fridge.

'Who else are you gonna talk to?'

'Well, you're not up for a civil conversation, are you?' She was surprised he was awake.

Tim shrugged as he poked through her food supplies in the fridge.

'You're not meant to be here, and I was quite prepared to hang with Bandit as my singing partner over the holidays. He never complains about my cooking.' She then wagged her finger at him. 'And don't think I'm here to pander to you either, your Highness. I'm not here to cook and clean for you, I'm doing it for me, and I've got work to do. And don't eat all my stuff either.'

'Take it and fly away with you. Email the stuff, I don't care. Just don't be here.' Tim dumped the milk back into the fridge then slapped the door shut.

'I have to be here.'

'Why?' He asked, heading back to his indented

couch.

'Because we have a contract and because you're not here.' He may be here in body—in a well-put-together body—but the man she adored wasn't there in spirit at all.

Tim scowled at her from over his shoulder and turned around to face her. He gave her a long, hard look, dragging his gaze from the top of her messy blonde head of hair to the pink polish on her bare toes. It was a look she felt everywhere—it completely exposed her.

Tim stepped forward, then stopped. 'Claude?'

She stood square, jutting her chin out. She wasn't giving in to this guy—even though she always did. Eventually.

'Take the money and run.'

'No. You take the ute and run. You can still catch a plane to Perth for the summer.'

He screwed his face up and pushed so hard on the kitchen's screen door it slammed against the wall. 'Like hell I'm gonna go and face that mob this year, not with their pity looks. I was supposed to be hanging out on a beach in Bali, but noooo everything got cancelled.' He ripped open the beer fridge and cracked open a can. Head back, his Adam's apple bobbled with each deep pull of the beer. Trickles of amber liquid spilled from the corners of his mouth and down his bare chest.

The guy was a heartbroken mess.

Monet eyed the clock on the wall as the kettle whistled. She wanted to say something, do something.

They were already playing the *art of snark* game that would soon build into a full-blown argument. No doubt she'd bite back and say something that would only make him feel worse. Then she'd beat herself up for the rest of her time here for hurting the poor guy.

Instead, she did what she always did—made her coffee strong and black, grabbed her tablet, slipped on her boots, and walked out the door.

She had a job to do, a contract to keep. At least she could control this part of her holiday plan.

In the office she opened the window to allow the morning air to filter into the musty room. She tidied up the piles of paperwork on the large oak desk, then wiped off the dust that lay in a fine film over the bare surfaces.

Competition blue ribbons, assorted medallions and various trophies and plaques were kept in the glass cabinet that ran along the wall. Alongside them were the many photos of Tim, with his dad, Jack Kirby, escorting their prize-winning cattle. They started with images of Tim as a boy, through his gawky teenage years, to the strong man standing shoulder to shoulder with his father. The proud pair of cattlemen, continuing a long-standing family tradition of breeding beautiful Brahman.

The overhead fan stirred the soupy air as she turned on the two-way radio and called in like she'd promised. 'Elsie Creek Tower… This is a whole load of double W's with a one. You there, Mickey?' Her handle was technically WW WW 1, but Mickey never bothered with details—

unless it came to flying and sweeping his airstrips. Besides everyone knew who she was.

'Go ahead, *Wicked Witch of the Westerly Winds*,' said Mickey with a crackle to his gravelly voice.

She'd checked in with him yesterday when putting Gertrude to bed, where the essential oils from Kat's candles still lingered in the plane. 'So, what's the goss of the day?'

'Have you taken a gander at the weather map yet? I tried to call you last night but couldn't get through?'

'No, I'm taking a peek at the BOM site now.' On her tablet, Monet scrolled through to the Bureau of Meteorology's website and tracking maps. 'So, they finally kissed?' Yesterday, two singular storm cells that were sitting in the Gulf of Carpentaria had now forged into one large tropical low. It was the start of a cyclone.

'They're predicting it'll be a category five, kid.'

'Where's it going to land?'

'Close, but you're grounded.'

'I'm what? It's too early for that, it's still on a watch.'

'Cos that National Disaster mob have been yakking all over the airways about diverting planes and closing airstrips all the way to Darwin.'

'What did they say?' Monet asked the man who practically had his ear glued to the airways 24/7, living beneath the biggest radio tower they had in town.

'Based on that cyclone's projection those tropical thermals will slam your light plane to earth so fast you'll be powerless to stop them. It's already churning up winds over 200 clicks.'

The screen door opened behind her.

Tim approached, peeking over her shoulder to gaze at her tablet.

'When are they predicting it'll make land?' Tim asked her.

She shrugged, and spoke into the microphone, 'Mickey, tell Marcus I'm here and so is Tim.' She frowned at Tim as she put the office phone back on the hook to charge.

'I didn't want anyone to disturb me,' Tim said, taking her tablet to zoom in on the BOM's reports.

'People have been trying to warn you, dickhead.' She scowled at him as she spoke into the radio's handpiece, 'Mickey, what are you doing in preparation?' Because it was a monster-sized storm.

'I'm strapping down planes. There are no other pilots about, they've all gone away for Christmas. But they're promising me a stack of beer for doin' the job. You do it too, kid. No slap happy boat anchor on Gertrude this time. I want full tie-downs and that means puttin' them pegs deep into the ground.'

'I could fly back and give you a hand,' she suggested.

Tim nodded with his back to her, seated at his desk staring at her tablet.

'No,' said Mickey's gravelly voice over the radio's speakers. 'You're grounded, kid. I'll go check on the Inn on my way to the pub later. Until then, you and Tim batten down. Call me later this arvie and keep that phone on the hook. Over and out.'

She returned the radio's microphone to its cradle and faced Tim. 'What's your cyclone plan for Rigby Downs?' The man had a plan for everything.

'Um…' Tim grabbed her coffee cup and took a deep mouthful as he focused on the weather map.

'Hey, that's mine.'

'Technically, it's my cup,' he said with a slight grin over the rim as he took another mouthful, obviously searching for sobriety.

'Want me to make more coffee?'

'In a thermos to go?'

'You can't drive.'

'Why not?'

'You'll still be over the limit from last night's little tea party for one.'

'My station.'

'Don't care. I'll drive and for once you can tell me what to do. If you're lucky, I might even listen to your instructions.'

'Oh, really?' Hands behind his head, his grin grew as he leaned back in his seat and crossed his legs at the ankles. 'And you'll do exactly as I say, eh?'

'Ugh, only after you've showered!' She pinched her nose and backed out the door. 'You go bathe and pretend to be human and think of a plan. I'll make food for the road, but our first stop is Gertrude, or I'll go now—'

'No.' He caught her arm before she got too far ahead, opening the kitchen door for her. 'We'll go together to make sure your plane's tied down. My fencing mallet's in the back of the ute. We'll need it to hammer those cables home. I'll go shower and…' He scrubbed his hair as if trying to wake himself up.

'How about a bacon and egg burger? Coffee rich, thick and black?'

'So, you're not a vegetarian?' His lips flickered into a grin as the light started to spark in his eyes.

'Not full time. It'd be a waste when on a cattle station, don't you think?' Monet replied cheekily.

Fully loaded, his grin was dynamite. It made her heart and temperature explode.

'Go, you're distracting me,' she said, pushing him toward the hallway.

'Thank you, Claude. I'll have pepper and barbecue sauce on that burger, with soft eggs if you can muster it.'

'You'll get what you're given. I'm not a cook on demand, like Master Chef Lucy.'

'How is the Station Hand's daughter?'

'Having the best time. She's got her own YouTube channel, doing cooking shows. Her parents are semi-retired and live with her now to help run their online bush herb business.'

'The legendary Station Hand is camping at the Unofficial Elsie Creek Inn?'

She laughed. 'Can you picture it? That man

complains about being claustrophobic in town.' The Station Hand was like an outback guru, paid to save cattle stations while training stockmen in their trade. He was the best in the biz.

'I'd take that as a no. So where is he?'

'The Station Hand and the lovely Liz, have their acreage. They're with Lucy, living with the new fire chief, Jax, at the Clare's old place. She's even engaged to be married to the guy.' She was so glad Lucy wasn't home alone at the Inn, and that Rigsy was safely out near Harts Range.

'Engaged?' And just like that all civility disappeared as the clouds shadowed his light blue eyes.

'You, shower. We've got a station to prepare.' She flicked her fingers in front of his face to wake him up. 'Focus, cowboy.'

He squinted at her, catching her hand, narrowing his eyes at her. 'I hate you right now.'

He looked like he hated the world.

'Whatever, blame me. Fire me when it's over, if that'll make you feel any better.' She pushed him towards the bathroom, not giving the grouch an excuse. If he'd been wallowing in his drinking stupor for a while, Tim was going to be one sick puppy when the hangover hit. But he needed to get his focus back, and fast, because he'd hate himself even more if he didn't do something to save his station today.

In the kitchen, Monet made breakfast and coffee. She

was listening to the radio's news when the phone rang. 'Rigby Downs,' she said, cradling the phone's handpiece between her ear and shoulder.

'Who's that?' demanded a female voice.

'The hired help. To whom do I have the pleasure of speaking with?' Why not, it was the Posh Prince's place—Mrs Kirby might even approve.

'This is Sherice.'

Monet dropped the phone with her face all screwed-up as if she'd eaten a dozen sour Kakadu plums.

'Hello? Hello… Anyone there?' Sherice's voice cried out like a ghost screeching through the speaker as the phone lay on the floor.

Monet stared down at the handpiece, so tempted to bash it flat with the saucepan.

The shower kept running in the background, and bacon sizzled on the grill.

'Hellooooooo!'

Picking up the phone and holding it in a death grip, Monet asked coolly, 'What do you want?'

'I want to talk to Timothy. Monet, is that you?'

The man's name is Tim. He only got called Timothy when he was in trouble, and Monet knew trouble when she heard it. 'The master of this mansion is busy right now.'

'Sugar, go and tell my man to get un-busy and talk to me right now. There's a cyclone coming.'

'We're well aware of that, thank you for your concern. Have a nice life.' Monet hung up, giggling.

But the phone only rang again.

'Rigby Do—'

'It didn't take you long to crawl over there, did it, Monet,' snarled Sherice. 'I'm not done. I must talk to Timothy.'

'Maybe he's choosing not to communicate with you at this time and point in space?'

'Huh? This is none of your concern. Now, fetch me Timothy—'

'Look, lady,' Monet said, rolling her eyes to the ceiling, 'is this call going to involve national security? Cos, unless the earth stops spinning, no one here wants to hear your dribble—'

'What?'

'Is. It. Important?'

'Of course, it is.'

'Why? Are you his bank manager? His lawyer?'

'I'm his soon-to-be—'

'EX,' Monet hissed over the phone. 'Can you say, *ex*? As in the past. Gone. Has been. Been there, done that, and should've kicked it kerbside a long time ago.'

'So says the woman who's slept with half of the stockmen in the Top End as the madam of your dumpy Inn.'

'Wow. I've been a busy girl, haven't I? All that time flat on my back, how on earth do I get any work done?'

'You don't work.'

'Says the girl with the perfect manicure and shiny

boots on Daddy's station. Listen, sweetness, as much as I'd love to keep this chin music up, I'm changing this playlist to busy. Call back next decade.' And she hung up, again.

Now she understood why Tim kept the phone off the hook.

At least he was off the couch and doing what he did best, managing his station.

Sure, she could fly out, no matter what Mickey said. She certainly wasn't letting some desk jockey stuck in some interstate office dictate to her the flying rules based on time-delayed weather reports. Most of them wouldn't even know where Elsie Creek was on the map.

She could see the weather conditions, and didn't mind taking risks to bend the rules to suit. Rules had never bothered her, because she didn't live by anyone's rules. Only her own.

But she wasn't leaving Tim, not until this threat was over.

Although she was unsure which was the bigger threat—the cyclone or Tim's ex, Sherice.

FIVE

Tim sat in the passenger seat of his ute like a guest on his own cattle station. He scoffed down his breakfast, trying to remember the last meal he'd eaten, or when he'd last bothered to shave. Let alone have a coffee handed to him with a handful of painkillers by the little pocket rocket.

His days had blurred into one looong drinking session. It was nothing more than beer and television.

Did he remember to feed his dog?

Over his shoulder, through the back window, he peered at the stocky Bandit standing sure-footedly on the back tray of his ute. The blue cattle dog's smile sparkled in his eyes with his ears pinned back facing the wind. His dog now followed Monet like most men did—until she left or told them to leave.

'When did you finish the shed?' Monet asked, pointing to the roof that reflected the sun's shine.

It hurt his eyes, so he lowered his Akubra's brim. 'A month ago. I used the money from…' He frowned, clearing his throat. 'Have you got any more painkillers?'

'Not for another two hours. You'll survive.'

His stomach rumbled from the aroma of bacon and barbecue sauce that had his mouth watering. He eyed the mountain of food sitting beside the thermos in his mum's old basket. 'Can I—'

'Yes. I cooked extra for you.' She didn't even bat an eyelid, keeping her eyes on the road, steering them toward the airstrip.

Monet was the only person on the planet who knew what he was thinking. It used to be annoying.

He snatched up another bacon burger and eagerly tucked in.

Their shoulders swayed as they shifted in their seats with the ute bouncing over deep corrugations on the track. It'd been a while since he'd checked the airstrip. Flashes of red stood out between the gaps in the gum trees. They soon fell away, opening to a monstrous skyline as the backdrop to her little red plane, shining in the sun.

He hadn't seen that plane in… well over a year.

Back then, it used to make him laugh whenever he'd see it fly overhead with its straw broom painted on the underbelly and music blaring from its speakers. Without fail, someone would call out, *'here comes the Wicked Witch of the Westerly Winds.'*

With Gertrude on the station, it was always a good couple of days. Monet would share her latest playlist, deliver the mail, balance their books, spreading cheer and brassy sass with her until she flew out at dawn.

Now, frowning at the silent plane, Tim couldn't remember the last time he'd been a passenger.

It used to be a regular thing.

Every year Monet would take Tim and his dad on aerial searches for their cattle and to check the tracks from the wet season floods to work out his mustering plan.

Then his dad died, and Monet stopped visiting.

But she was here now.

Parking under the corrugated lean-to's shade, Monet went straight to her plane. She patted its sturdy wings like a horseman approached their steed.

She loved her plane.

It would have to be the only thing Monet loved, because the woman was a proper minimalist, and had been since the day he'd met her. She never fussed over clothes, or fashion trends. Her passions were music, her plane, and her knack for numbers.

But that little red plane did countless miles with its cheeky, husky-voiced bush pilot. They delivered mail, doing bookwork, conducting aerial cattle searches and crop dusting for many stations. Monet even played the part of flying taxi, commuting people from outstations and communities into town for doctor days. The woman spent more time in the air than on the ground, and would rather be anywhere else other than hanging at her home.

Whereas Rigby Downs was Tim's home; he'd never leave if he didn't have to.

Screeching rainbow lorikeets whizzed overhead, flashing their orange-and-red underwings as they shifted from tree to tree. The humid air was thick with sweet honey from flowering natives bursting with colour, he could smell the lush green growth.

Tim loved the wet season on the station. It was when the sunburnt dust finally settled under the rain, making every man and beast sigh with relief. The musters were over and it was his time to kick back in his fishing boat and watch the migratory water birds glide across the flood plains.

He didn't mind watching the birds. There was a multitude of varieties and they were so free. They reminded him of Monet and the thrill she got from flying.

He got that same rush every time he chased the monsoonal storm clouds. He'd race toward the rain in his air boat, with its aircraft-type propeller pushing the flat-bottomed boat to skim over a vast inland sea that reflected a titanic, oceanic blue skyline. It was his excuse to check the water levels along the fence lines or stock routes. He was always looking for a chance to fly on land.

But he'd done none of that this year, except crash on the couch to watch cricket and drink beer.

'What's happening with the Unofficial Elsie Creek Inn?' Tim asked, digging around the back of his ute.

'Mickey's going to take a look at the place later.' Keeping her hand on Gertrude's smooth shell, Monet inspected the plane the way a horseman inspects their mount before riding. 'Rigsy and I did a cyclone clean-up a month ago. We timed it for Train Day and put on a barbecue. The Caveman even rocked up and took command of the barbecue. It went for days with someone new showing up with more beer and steak every couple of hours. It's easy to see how the Caveman won King of the Billabong Bake-off again. Oh hey, Lucy won the title of Queen; I was so proud of her.'

'Lucy? For real?' As best friends those two girls were polar opposites. Lucy was such a shy thing compared to the outspoken pocket rocket.

'You should've come.' Monet retrieved a roll of cables from the belly hatch of the plane and slipped on some thick leather fencing gloves.

'I'd forgotten it was on.' Tim didn't feel like being civil to anyone. Yet, a part of him missed the fun he would've had, the Elsie Creek Billabong Barbie Bash was always a superb day.

'Do you need pegs?' Tim asked, grabbing his own sturdy roping gloves and mallet. 'I've got some long posts spare. That way you can tell Mickey you did as you were told—for once.'

'If you're offering. The ground's soft enough from the

rain, it shouldn't take too much for you to play pretend strong man, hammering them home.'

'Are you gonna ring the bell and give me a prize, as the ringmaster of your own private circus?'

'I don't do bells, especially this time of year.'

'I don't miss those in the carols that get played over and over,' he said, hauling half a dozen star pickets over his shoulder with a mallet in hand.

Monet pulled out a tarp, some cargo net, and dumped them near the tyres. She then started wrapping them up like terrible Christmas presents.

'What are you doing?'

'Dingoes. I heard them last night and these are new tyres.'

'Are the pups' still trying to chew on them? Dad used to spray them with a homemade chilli oil, they soon learned.'

'I'll remember that for the future. Beats me why, when they don't chew on utes, only plane tyres.'

'You've changed to mud tyres?'

'It helps for the wet season.' Monet fastened the rope tight around the bulky package of the plane's legs, then started dragging out more thick cables from the open belly hatch. 'I'm thinking of getting some of those amphibious floats to turn Gertrude into a part-time sea witch.'

'Gertrude wouldn't handle the leg weight, she's not a seaplane.'

'Of course, she can. We just couldn't find anything

red to match her wardrobe,' she said with a straight face, but he had to laugh at the glimmer in her eyes.

With the plane tied down, they cruised along the station's many tracks. They opened gates, unclipped solar electric fences and removed batteries to the back of his ute. Sheeting and bore pumps were also shifted as they tried to limit the debris that could turn into potential missiles.

At the end of the last muster, Tim had shifted the cattle to higher ground to let them fatten up over the wet season. It's what he did every year before letting the station hands go for the summer.

It was then up to the storm, with Tim busily planning on the damage assessments he'd need to make afterwards.

He turned down the music to ask, 'What else is happening in Elsie Creek?'

Monet drove them over the crest towards the homestead. The new shed's shiny roof didn't annoy him, now that he was on his second lot of painkillers, with only crumbs left in Monet's basket of goodies and a full stomach.

'The town's adopted this cranky old croc and called it Karma,' she said, while skilfully unwrapping a red and white candy cane and popping it into her mouth. 'They rescued it from Jax and Lucy's dam. He's missing a foot and wouldn't have survived long in the wild. So the Station Hand and his groupies built this fancy pen for the crocodile, in the pub's beer garden. Karma predicted the AFL Grand Final winner and the Melbourne Cup winner.'

She frowned, sucking on her hard candy cane.

Leaning closer to the steering wheel she peered up at the sky covered with grey patchy clouds.

'And?'

'Karma predicted this cyclone.'

Tim frowned. 'How? It's a crocodile. Not a psychic.'

'Try telling that to the mob who feed the thing. Remember those wishing wells, where you toss a coin to make a wish?'

'Yeah.'

'These guys hold up two pieces of meat on a long pole with the question taped over the top. They dangle it over the crocodile, and whichever one the croc chooses to eat is the winner. It works every time.'

'Bull.'

'See for yourself, you'll crack up laughing. The pub's making a fortune out of it with all these people wanting to pay the pub to feed the pub's pet crocodile. I don't know how long it'll last, though? I heard the new ranger telling the Station Hand that Karma needs to go on a diet, but when it comes to the Station Hand and conversation—'

'Yeah, he talks and everyone listens kind of conversation.'

'The new ranger's tough. I like her,' said Monet with a wicked grin. 'You should have seen her stand up to the Station Hand and his groupies. I had to remind them that they need to be nice to the new ranger because she's the one issuing the permit to allow them to keep that crocodile in the pub.'

'A fortune-telling crocodile called Karma.' Tim chuckled, wiping at the gritty layer of dust on his face. This would have to be the most conversation he'd had with anyone since…

'It's a brilliant name,' Monet said, steering his ute like she owned it. 'Karma's got quite a following, and his own Instagram account. The tourists are stopping in for lunch on their way to Kakadu.'

'I bet that's why the publican has agreed to keep it.'

'My rock-climbing buddy is cool, and looking forward to her day off.'

'Yeah, Samantha only shuts the pub on Christmas Day. Hey, what do you do on Christmas?'

'Nothing. I'll wallow in the bathtub and sing to Bandit. Christmas is just a normal day for me, it doesn't exist.'

'Is that why you've always volunteered to farm sit?'

'Your Dad understood why.'

Tim did too. They just never spoke about it.

'Your mother enjoyed the fact I got to pack away all of her Christmas decorations.'

'Mum always said that was the one good thing about having you farm-sit for the summer.'

'It'd be the only thing she liked about me,' mumbled Monet, sucking on her candy cane like it was a cigar. 'So, your mother took all her decorations and furniture with her?'

'Yep. Mum's got herself a neat little unit near the

beach in Esperance. She loves it. The aunts are just down the road.'

'I'm surprised your mother hasn't come back to take care of her little prince.'

'Claude, we've been playing so nicely,' he warned her.

She aimed that wicked grin at him, it was like a shotgun blast of heat into his chest. He had to lower his hat's brim and look away.

'Mum can't handle the heat anymore, her ankles swell. Besides, I don't want her in my space.' He sighed, staring out at the green fields that blended with the trees into one never-ending sea of green. 'Mum wants me to get back with Sherice.'

'Sherice rang while you were in the shower—oh shoot!' She waved her candy cane in the air like a wand. 'I forgot to put the phone back on the hook.'

They grinned at each other.

'You know, honey, as much as I love you,' she said with that sad look that stared deep into his soul.

He cringed as she parked his ute under the cover of his new shed, where the temperature dropped a few degrees. He liked his new sturdy cyclone-coded shed. It had plenty of room to store his toys.

'I have to tell you,' Monet said in a tone loaded with sorrow, 'heartbreak is like an ice cream shop, it has many flavours—'

'I suppose you've tasted them all.'

'I've had double scoops, cos I'm greedy.' Popping the candy cane back in her mouth, she gave his arm a squeeze. 'You'll survive this and you'll be so much stronger for it.'

'Like you. The cold-hearted witch who flies away from any form of emotional attachment.'

'Do not.'

'You do too. Name one guy you've dated—actually dated.' He raised his hand. 'I'm not judging, nor do I believe for a second all those rumours of you and the ringers. I know you wouldn't lower your standards to most of them. Go on, admit it, you don't date.'

'Sure. So what? But I don't look at men or women like cattle in a stockyard either.'

'What do you mean by that?' Tim asked her.

'You, who's all about selective breeding and genetics.'

'I breed blue ribbon worthy beef.'

'And that's how you like your women.'

'Bull.'

'Go on, admit it. Your reptilian brain started screaming at you to breed, so you started this whole carefully scripted five-year campaign as part of your personal genetic breeding program. Where's the love? Where's the passion and spontaneous—'

'Where's the part about her cheating on me? ME! What did I do?'

'It's not you who is to blame, it's her. So stop blaming yourself, okay,' she said. 'Hey, sometimes you just have to accept that life is chaotic and messy. It can't be planned down to the absolute micro-second.'

'I like being prepared—I just wasn't prepared for…'

'Sometimes those battlefields can be beautiful and wild too.'

'What?' He screwed his nose at her. 'Did you sneak a cocktail into your coffee cup?'

'I'm saying, sometimes the unplanned can be exciting. Besides, never underestimate the strength and courage you'll find as a survivor, living with a broken soul.'

'Like you?'

She shared a wry grin with a glimmer in her eyes. It was intimately addictive. 'Maybe letting people think I'm broken keeps away all those I don't need in my life.'

Her words cut through him, they made sense. How did she do that?

Monet leaned in closer.

He could smell the spearmint candy cane she held like a cigarette between her fingers.

'A crisis doesn't create character, it builds it, babe,' she said. 'Just think of all that free time you'd have for yourself if you didn't plan for everything.'

'I have to plan for work—unlike you who lives day to day.'

'Ah, but then I'm not disappointed if the plan never comes through. Am I?'

Her words, her comebacks, and answers for everything, sprang out of her like a quick recoiling nail gun, like normal. It used to amuse him, today he hated her for it, because this time her words were hitting him hard in the chest, forcing him to sit back and think.

'You were too good for Sherice, and she knows it. That's why she's crawling back,' Monet said so matter-of-factly, scooping up the empty food basket and travel mugs, then climbing out of the ute.

'You're crazy.' And ticking him off with her blasé know-it-all attitude.

'I'm freaking insane, that's how everyone else sees me.' She closed the door and leaned down through the open window.

The candy cane rolling across her tongue was a seductive song. It matched that impossible smile and shiny eyes that cracked through the walls of his soul.

'That's why I don't bother dating. I don't want to have any children.'

Tim wanted lots of kids. 'But you love kids.' Monet would make an amazing mother. 'And kids love you.'

'My genetics are so freaking not-normal. I'm not damning my kids to that kind of torture.'

His heart dropped to the floormats of his ute, feeling her pain.

She pushed away from the window, leaving him still seated in his ute. 'I'll do the cyclone prep around the house. You do your sheds. Oh, by the way, my mother is fine, thanks for asking.' She tossed the basket over her shoulder and swaggered away.

The diesel engine ticked as it cooled down, matching the scents of assorted fuels and oils from the silent machinery. Tim watched Monet's sexy swagger through the mirror as she headed back to the house with Bandit hot on her heels.

She was wrong.

She was crazy.

And she was doing his head in.

She was maddeningly all things sugar and spice and everything nice, with a sharp tongue, a powerful will and tonnes of sex appeal.

But Monet was also right. *Bitch*.

He hated how she was right. There were no sugar-coated niceties with Monet. It was buckle up and get your butt kicked black and blue on the home-grown truths of Monet's life lessons.

Tim would look at logistics and footholds, busily planning back-up contingencies as part of the bigger picture. While Monet was the type to run headlong into a storm, waving her over-flowing cocktail glass in the air, ready to dance in muddy puddles.

It surprised him she was still here helping him prepare for this storm.

He peered to the horizon with its grey skies, thickening with rain. Unfortunately, it didn't ease the high humidity.

It wasn't the incoming storm that bothered him; they were only under a cyclone watch. It hadn't upgraded to a cyclone warning yet, which gave him time. He had insurance, and his machinery was packed away in his new shed so he wasn't too bothered about the storm itself.

It was the flooding that came afterwards that bothered him more.

The last time the floods came, people died. Two were from Monet's family.

SIX

Hands on hips, Monet scowled at the large lounge room with its walls of windows covered by heavy curtains. Thick layers of dust rested on every bare surface. Empty beer cans were piled near over-full beer boxes. The couch, thankfully vacant, had a body print indented into the cushions.

The guy used to be so house proud.

Tim was the type of guy who would lay out a clean towel before he'd let a lady sit on a dusty chair. He'd open doors for you, hold out your chair, give you the shirt off his back while finding you a hat so you didn't get sunburnt.

He used to be that guy.

As a meticulous planner, the guy had a place for

everything and everything in its place. He'd wear the same style of dress to not waste time on wardrobe choices. He preferred to have his mind on other things; that used to be all about Rigby Downs.

Treading over the beer cans, Monet opened the curtains to a glorious view of the sun rising over the station. The scene was a breath-taking vista of wide-open fields of gentle green slopes, with thick lush pockets of trees that stretched into the shadows on the distant horizon. After a dry and dusty winter, this summer's wet season had everything looking so vibrantly fresh and green.

The cyclone was sucking in the weather, leaving abnormally clear skies with the humidity shimmering like a blanket of fine water rising to meet the sun. She breathed in the steamy sauna air—it was putrid.

And it was coming from this room.

In the kitchen she flicked on the electric kettle, fed the dog, and paused before putting on the radio. Did she dare blast her music?

She was supposed to be home alone. Free to do her own thing—after she'd done the chores, then she could enjoy her holiday.

Not this tiptoeing around the place for his royal highness.

And that needed to stop, today.

She stomped down the hallway to the first stop on the rehab tour and banged on the closed bedroom door. 'Tim? Are you sleeping on the job again?'

Nothing.

She hammered her knuckles harder across the solid door panel.

'Go away,' came the muffled cry.

'I can't.' She flung open the door and trod over jeans and shirts to rip open his curtains. Daylight streamed through the window like a Hollywood red carpet spotlight to shine over the bed of tangled linen, making his highness the star of the show. 'Remember, I'm grounded.'

Tim hid under his pillow. 'Don't care. Go away.'

'No. Don't you think it's time you got up—'

'And do what?' With a fierce expression, he flung back the covers and scrambled off the bed.

She stepped back from the guy. Eyes widening as her jaw dropped.

He was naked.

Completely, beautifully, buck naked.

Thank the gods.

'Remember, I'm the boss and I'm on freaking holidays!' Tim slammed the curtains together so hard they waved on their rods as if suffering through a violent storm on a ship.

'But we've got—'

'We're still only on a cyclone watch, so I'm not getting my butt out of bed unless it gets upgraded.' Tirade finished, he belly-flopped onto the mattress, face down.

She gazed at his splendid buttocks, so tempted to slap on those beautiful butt cheeks like a set of bongos. They sat perfectly at the top of his thick athletic thighs, and as the base to his sculptured back muscles. Who knew she had a thing for back muscles—until now.

'Get out, Monet. Go play elsewhere. Or go and do what I pay you to do.' He shoved the pillow over his head.

Arsehole!

Sure, she might be staff, but she wasn't being paid to nursemaid the world's grumpiest boss either.

Lips tightened as her eyes narrowed in on the fine specimen of male laid out on the bed before her. But she never slept with her friends.

Right now—they weren't even friends.

She hurled the door shut behind her and stomped down the corridor. 'I'll do what I'm paid to do, shall I?' *This was war!*

In the kitchen, her phone sat on the counter with her small speaker. Monet scrolled through her playlists for something to suit her mood. She wanted heart-pumping, pulse-raging, ear-splitting, grumpy-boss-enraging workout music. The kind that would have a gym class collapsing with exhaustion.

The selection found, and *boom*—the ceiling practically bounced to Linkin Park. Live. In. Concert.

She grabbed the broom and did what she always did—finish all the crappy jobs first. And that meant cleaning this house.

Then she'd hit holiday mode.

Although this wasn't much of a holiday. Playing the

part of a lowly housemaid to the master-ogre of the house, who was impersonating sleeping beauty in his filthy pit.

What happened? He seemed fine yesterday. After their big day out, Tim ate, showered and collapsed into bed before sunset, leaving her home alone. So, what changed?

Beer cans clanged like cymbals being bashed at by a tone-deaf drummer, as she swept them into a pile by the front door. Music pumped from the tiny speaker in the kitchen so loud it had the table vibrating.

Until it got switched off.

'DO YOU MIND?' Tim shouted with that filthy look on his face, wearing a pair of crumpled dirty jeans that he'd probably found on the floor.

'Hey, look who finally got out of bed,' she replied. 'You look shorter without your hat on.'

He towered over her, giving off some serious shade. 'Just what the hell do you think you're doing?'

'What you're paying me to do, Your Highness. I'm cleaning *your* mess.' She even curtsied. If he dared call her Cinderella, she'd whack him with her broom.

'Huh?' With squinty eyes, he gave her a long look, taking in all the details from the top of her head to the bottom of her broom's bristles.

She couldn't breathe under that kind of scrutiny.

'Keep up the good work, then. Just clean quietly, please.' He snatched a water bottle from the fridge and the painkillers from on top. It was soon followed by his bedroom door slamming shut.

Wanker. She gripped the broom tight, tempted to sweep up the cans and dump them all over his bed.

Come on, she didn't even clean the Unofficial Elsie Creek Inn and here she was playing house for the Posh Prince who was sulking in bed.

Fine. She could play the game and there were many ways to scale a fish for frying and, baby, she was just getting started.

With headphones on and her music drowning out her thoughts, she sang at the top of her lungs as she filled the wheelbarrow with empty cans from the lounge room.

Then it was time to tackle an ancient beast she hated using. It rattled and wheezed, but most of all, it was loud.

It was the vacuum cleaner.

Today, she was going to do the best-damned vacuum ever, even if it took all day.

She vacuumed the lounge, the couch, the curtains and the cobwebs. She even did the windows; the fly screens and all the air-conditioner vents got sucked clean too.

She wrestled with the beastly thing like it was a writhing sea monster on land. Its bulky head banged loudly against the walls, skirting boards and doors, through the kitchen then down the corridor, sucking up all sorts of vagrant dust bunnies. Finally, and most gratifyingly, she hit door number one. The last room in the house.

Monet didn't even bother waiting for an answer before starting to vacuum his room.

There was a movement behind her and the machine

stopped sucking.

Tim held the separated power cords in hand. 'Get out!'

'I was just—'

'GET OUT.'

'Fine.' She dropped the hose, stepped over the silenced vacuum cleaner, and left it there lying in his room as he slammed the door behind her.

The house phone rang.

'Not my phone,' she tossed over her shoulder as she headed into the bathroom to wipe down the benches.

The house phone kept ringing in the kitchen.

'MONET, ANSWER THE PHONE.'

'ANSWER IT YOURSELF! I'm not your secretary, I'm busy playing housekeeper cleaning your bathroom. Hey, when did you get a new bathtub?' It was big enough for two people with jets. It looked amazing.

Meanwhile, the phone kept ringing.

Every step Tim took down the corridor towards the kitchen was like an ogre, full of fury, had been unleashed inside the house.

'Yeah,' he said over the phone, his voice trailing down the hallway.

Good, he's up.

Smiling to herself, she wiped down the sink and the mirror until it sparkled.

Tim came up behind her, with black rings under dull eyes and a five o'clock shadow that only highlighted his hollowed cheekbones. The guy who used to be a glowing picture of health, was now a mere shadow.

'It's for you,' he said, flipping up the lid on the toilet and unbuttoning his jeans.

'Huh?' She removed her earphones.

'The phone. It's for you. Do you mind? I'd like to pee in peace?'

'Who'd be calling me?'

'Cowboy freaking Craig.'

'Craig?' He was the last person she'd expected to call her, unless there was a problem with Sandy?

'You're not doing Craig, are you? That rodeo clown has got to be the biggest skirt chaser in the Territory.'

'Doing Craig? Well aren't you a Prince Charming, Timothy Kirby? Anyway, who I choose to be with is none of your business,' she said over her shoulder, leaving Mr Grumpy to do his business.

'Hello, Craig? Have you run out of beer already?' Monet said over the phone, reaching for a water bottle from the fridge. Hmm, she might have to top up her supplies shortly.

'I was thinking about driving out there and keeping you company for this storm,' said Craig, 'but Tim's there.'

'He is. Apparently, Tim lives here.'

'I CAN HEAR YOU!' Tim hollered from the bathroom.

'How's Sandlot Sandy?' She asked Craig, ignoring his highness in the hallway.

'Panicking about his place.'

'Are you driving back?'

'Well, we were gonna coerce the flying vet to play pilot but, like you, he's grounded and making his way through this fancy scotch he brought out.'

'Trying to be posh, is he?'

'We know he's not. Listen lovely, all is good on our end. We've got Sandy's neighbour peeking over the fence for a bit and I'm ringing to let you know that you can call me if you need anything. They've put in some new tower near Mum's, so I'm actually in mobile phone range. See, we're all good here. Now for the million-dollar question, are you?'

'I'm doing great.'

'Tim's damned lucky he's got you out there. Is he all right?'

'He's a little under the weather.'

'Yeah, that Sherice, huh?' Craig sighed.

She could picture Craig running his fingers through his blonde curls then readjusting his hat.

'See, that's why I don't do relationships, like you,' he said.

'I do my best to avoid relationships that lead to heartbreak, thank you very muchly.'

'And heartbreak hurts a tonne.'

Wow, that was a rare confession from the cowboy who broke lots of hearts. 'Are you okay?'

'You know me…'

Yeah, she did, but not the way most people thought either. 'Is the Christmas season stirring up stuff, huh?' Why did Christmas have to poke the ghosts of Christmas past for so many people?

'See, if you were nearby, I'd shout you some brekkie.'

'Well, I'm flicking the kettle on at my end.'

'I'm gonna crack my first brekkie beer. I am on holiday, you see.'

'I won't be far from making holiday cocktails too, once I finish the chores. So, tell me, what's going on?' She made her coffee and did what she did best for her friends, and that was listen while the house remained silent.

'And that's enough for today, huh?' Craig said, giving a nervous chuckle.

'Feel better?'

'Always. Now I'm gonna go and be the life of this cyclone party.'

'Good boy. Keep up the good work and give the flying vet a nudge for me.'

'I will, only after I've hidden his scotch on him.'

'You play nice.'

'Never. You stay out of trouble, if you can. If you can't be good, be good at it.'

'I aim to please.' She smiled, hanging up the phone.

Now, if only Tim would just open up to her, she was positive it'd help him too.

She scrolled through her emails. Last night she'd replied to lots of people who'd been checking up on her, to tell them she wasn't alone and all was okay. Her cousin Rigsy was keen to drive back to Elsie Creek or to the station to hang with her too.

She checked the BOM's weather site. The tropical low was teasing everyone. Sitting off the coast, sucking in all the clouds and ocean water, it was getting bigger every hour, brewing into a colossal storm.

At the best of times, cyclones were so unpredictable. No one knew when it would become a cyclone, and if it would crash the coast or head inland and become a much-needed rain depression.

'You and Craig, huh?' Tim said behind her, grabbing the milk from the fridge.

'Just mates.' Why should Tim care?

He drank from the carton, watching her. Again it trapped her on the spot.

Did he care?

'I'm going back to bed.' Slapping the fridge shut, he lazily dragged his feet down the hall, banging the bedroom door behind him.

She narrowed her eyes in his direction. *Well, I'm not done.*

She snatched up her hat and booted open the back door.

A simple lawn belt, that acted as a firebreak, ran around the house. A small orchard led to the chook pen and vegie patch, and that was pretty much it.

The Kirby men didn't house-garden. They didn't

need to, not with the amazing views they had of the expansive property. With the scattering of sheds, the rest was open land that stretched in all directions to meet the sky. There was nothing and no one else around.

She understood why the Kirby men preferred to be out on the station while Mrs Kirby stayed home cleaning the inside all day long.

And Monet was over cleaning. That part of the job she could tick off her contract.

But she wasn't ready to hide in the air-conditioned office to finish the books just yet—not while she had a game to play.

As Monet stalked across the grass to the small garden shed, half a dozen lean, grey brolgas flew overhead. Sleek, with wide wings, they had a lazy, graceful gliding style that made her smile.

She searched the sky for her favourite, the mighty expansive wing spread of the powerful sea eagle. Instead, there were galahs charging through the treetops like rookie pilots on training wheels. On the seed-end of leaning grasses, tiny zebra finches were quick and flighty, like muster choppers cutting off a rogue cleanskin.

She didn't mind playing the part of chief pilot for helicopter mustering teams. The physical and mental challenge in the low-flying aerial mustering of cattle was like living on daily doses of adrenalin shots. No two days were the same in the short-term seasonal work, with unplanned hours from four days to four weeks out in the scrub. But with her plane she flew all year round doing the mail run, with a guaranteed couple of weeks off for her annual Christmas hideaway holiday.

But this didn't feel like a holiday—stuck playing the part of the freaking underpaid staff member with the sucky job of babysitting the grumpy boss.

Monet glanced back at the house. Wearing an evil grin, she yanked back the cord and the beastly behemoth of all noises erupted.

Birds scurried for cover as it spluttered, coughed and spewed a thick cloud of black smoke until it found its lungs. The body rattled like a thousand freight trains barrelling down a dilapidated railway line.

Headphones on, she cranked up the volume, adjusted her hat and sunnies, gripped the rusty handlebar and pushed the rattling contraption through the grass.

She'd never been so happy to mow the lawn, until now.

SEVEN

He hated her. Never in his life did Tim hate anyone more than Monet, right now.

The crusty old lawnmower was battering a hundred jackhammer drills into the side of his head. Dying of thirst, his mouth was like sandpaper. The same sandpaper that left a tonne of grit behind his closed eyelids.

He'd suffered hangovers before, but not like this. Was he suffering alcohol poisoning from his liquid diet of beer too?

In dire need of water, he stumbled from the bed. Empty plastic water bottles crinkled under his feet, between his clothes.

'OW.' The shooting pain from his foot only topped

off the headache, while he was forced to dance in the dark holding onto his stubbed toe.

Flicking on the light, he scowled down at the vacuum cleaner. 'MONET?'

The damned house phone rang. Again.

Well, isn't this day off to a magical start!

Limping, while wincing at the bright light inside the house, he made his way down the hall. He'd kept the place hidden behind closed curtains, which were now open, and spotlessly clean. To add to his pain, the polished floors reflected the sunlight streaming through the open front door and shiny windows.

He'd never realised how big this house was without the furniture cluttering it all up.

But the stupid house phone just kept ringing and ringing.

He sneered at the thing he wanted to tear off the wall. 'What!'

'Is this Rigby Downs?' Asked the male voice on the other end of the phone line.

'Yeah, what of it?'

'Tim? Is that you?'

'Who's this?'

'It's Marcus.'

'Oh, hey Marcus. Sorry mate, I was expecting someone else.'

'Are you all right?'

'I'm suffering a delayed hangover.'

'Lucky you.' Marcus chuckled.

'What's up, Sarge? Are you looking for an excuse to skip town and go fishing out at one of my billabongs?'

'After Christmas, I'll take you up on the offer for sure. I'm after Monet.'

'Monet?'

'Yeah, is she around?'

'She's mowing my lawn.'

'No way?'

Tim heard Marcus smile, which was indeed a rare thing for the town's top cop.

'I don't believe it! You'll have to take some photos for me.'

'She is. By hand.' What was wrong with his ride-on? Tim liked that toy, where he'd cruise around with beer in hand, admiring the smell of freshly cut grass.

'I'll have to get Monet to mow mine when she's finished her contract out there,' said Marcus.

Tim frowned as an unexpected heated rage rumbled from his lower chest, clenching his teeth. 'I'll go get Monet for you and you can ask her yourself.' He dropped the phone onto the bench, in such a foul mood, the anger twisted inside him the way a whirly whirly throws dust around.

'OI. PHONE.' He shouted to Monet, glaring at her pushing his mower.

Thankfully, she silenced the rattletrap.

'Who is it?' Monet asked.

'You might want to brush up your Tinder game, because I've got your boyfriend going on about cutting his grass.'

'My what?'

'Do me a favour? Please unplug my phone when you're done. It's not Monet's party line, it's my phone and I'm sick of playing secretary when I'm the one who's the boss around here.'

The hot sun hurt his eyes. His entire body ached from walking the length of the lawn that was like hiking the entire Kakadu Highway. With his teeth clenched, he stropped through the kitchen and snatched up another bottle of water from the fridge.

Thankfully, Monet had filled it with food and water she'd carted in with her.

'Bugger.' He head-butted the fridge shut.

I'm such a selfish bastard.

He'd been eating Monet's food, which was her means of survival for the next few weeks. It's why she was cleaning and mowing, their contract required her to take care of the farmhouse.

Every summer, they'd always come back from holidays to a clean house, mowed lawn and books done. He would also drive back home carting a load of food to keep them going for a month.

When only a few days ago he'd been staring at his bare cupboards, eating cold baked beans straight from the can. Now, there were exotic foods sitting beside milk cartons, coffee, and a fridge full of food. Most of which he didn't know how to pronounce, let alone cook.

'Hello?' Monet said on the phone behind him.

Is she sleeping with Marcus?

'Oh, hey Marcus, I was just thinking about you.'

Yep! She is.

Tim rolled his eyes, too sore to shake his head and stumbled back to his bedroom.

Monet and Marcus. Well, that'd work much better than Cowboy Craig and Monet. Their town's top cop was tough enough to rein in the pocket rocket should she head for trouble.

It's what Tim used to do for her.

But now he'd been replaced by a bigger, broader, musclier guy who carried a gun and could control a room of brawling blokes with just one look—cos the man had a set of knuckles that hit like a sledgehammer and he wasn't afraid to use them.

But Marcus also didn't want a relationship. In charge of a police station, Marcus always said he was too busy with work, having too much fun playing with the ladies to be in any kind of serious relationship.

Tim knew this because Marcus was his fishing partner.

What did Monet see in Marcus? She could do better than that buffed-up beefcake.

In fact, no one was good enough for his Monet.

His Monet... The words rolled around his brain

sending a wave of soothing warmth through his chest.

Most men felt challenged having a dare-devil for a girlfriend.

Most men didn't like a smart-mouthed, cocktail-making beauty with brains, who saw straight through people and wasn't afraid to say so. Or worse, if she didn't want to talk to you, she'd walk away, giving the best view of her sexy swagger that always made his head tilt to watch.

She was trouble. She was chaos. She was passion. Most of all, she felt like home to him.

Monet's shock of laughter brought him up short. It was nothing like the husky purr he'd expected from her if she was talking to her boyfriend. This was clear and bright.

Tim wanted to hear her husky purr and have it aimed at him.

He frowned at the closed door in her direction.

She was talking to Marcus. Not him.

She was laughing with Marcus, and not him.

What did Marcus have that he didn't have?

'Whoa!' The realisation of what his mind was doing made him sit hard on his bed, staring at the pile of jeans on the floor.

Why, when, what?

Could he be jealous of Marcus for making Monet laugh?

Tim couldn't remember the last time he'd made Monet smile. A smile that used to make him want to smile with her, let alone laugh together.

They used to have so much fun. All the time.

Carrying on conversations over nothing that would have them shedding happy tears holding their sides from stitches.

His dad used to say Tim and Monet matched each other like beer-battered fish went with hot crispy chips.

But did they?

No. This couldn't be happening? Not when another woman had already crushed his soul.

Collapsing onto the bed, Tim hid his head under the pillow, defeated.

There was a knock on the door.

Ugh. How long was she going to keep torturing him?

Tim threw back his pillow in anger and blinked at the clock. He must have dozed off. But the smell of food had his stomach churning.

There was another knock.

'*What?*' He stumbled out of bed, side-stepped the vacuum cleaner and yanked open the door.

But there was no one there.

On the floor stood a tray full of food, accompanied by a pineapple wearing sunglasses.

'What the—?'

He plucked the note wedged in between the fronds of the pineapple's prickly head:

This is a peace pineapple!
He's a token of sunshine and good times ahead
and he's here to help you fight your penance.
He brings pain pills along with food fit for a

*king and an amazing bloody Mary to take the
edge off your hangover.
Eat, sleep, and forget about being merry for the
day.
I'll talk to you tomorrow… Maybe.
Monet. XOXO
PS, this food delivery service is a one-time-only
deal, Princess.*

He looked up and down the hallway. The place was quiet. There were no lawnmower noises. No music. No singing or cooking noises. His ute stood out the front and the house phone was unplugged.

He glanced at the pineapple with its sweet fragrance and coarse skin beneath the prickly green top. The pineapple's sunglasses reflected his cheesy grin. 'Peace pineapple, huh?'

A truce.

A smug smirk matched his puffed-out chest.

It didn't last long. He felt hollow, spurred on by the food's aroma that had hunger clawing at his ribs.

Scooping up the tray and peace pineapple, he closed his door, pleased he'd won this round of their snark game, and he was once again the boss of this house.

But had he truly won?

Not when he'd lost time… days even.

He'd even lost his pride.

Had he lost his best friend too?

EIGHT

The woman was loud. Lots of differing versions of loud. From clomping her boots down the hallway, or clanking plates and cups in the kitchen, to full on blasting her stereo in the office. How Monet worked with all that racket was beyond him.

The noise that bothered Tim the most was when she was having her own dance parties—with *his* dog, on *his* verandah—and *he* wasn't invited.

Tim wasn't that sick to not listen to Monet singing while cooking in the kitchen either. The cooking aromas were divine and her meals were magnificent and he'd told her so. So how did she repay his compliments?

By telling him he had to wash the dishes.

His dishes. In *his* house. By *his* staff.

Technically, she was his paid bookkeeper and farm-sitter, doing an exceptional job. But Monet wasn't just the hired help. She would have flown out of here in a flat second if she had wanted to leave. No, Monet just didn't want to go back to the big empty Inn or leave him alone with this storm. He knew that much about the woman.

So today, Tim attempted to play nice. Even getting up, showering and making breakfast before Monet stumbled out of her room with her soft, tousled mop of dirty blonde hair and sleepy eyes, wearing just a damned T-shirt. It was sexy as hell.

Shame it wasn't his T-shirt.

Enough! He had to stop thinking about Monet like this. They'd been in the friend zone a long time. Longer than any other friend he had.

Nope, he would not ruin something that was balancing precariously on a very rocky surface at the moment, and so he chose to stay out of her way for the day.

It was late in the afternoon when he grabbed his Akubra off the hook by the kitchen door. He held onto the door frame as he slipped on his boots, well trained to not track dirt through the house, considering all the effort Monet had put into cleaning the place.

Music travelled from somewhere in the yard.

The last he'd seen of his once-hostile house-sitter was when she'd dragged in a load of fruit earlier this morning. Bananas and pawpaw accompanied another peace pineapple Tim didn't even know he was growing.

Monet had also found a huge stash of eggs she'd made into breads and cakes while talking to his dog. Not him, the station owner, but his dog, Bandit.

The outdoors-only working dog had truly hit happy holiday mode. Bandit, the sneaky bugger, even had a spot under the kitchen table getting handfed morsels by Monet.

Tim shouldn't be complaining. With assorted baked goods presently cooling across his kitchen counters, Monet had kept him company while also having that knack of keeping her distance, giving him that room to breathe… and sulk.

Mind you, Monet always kept her distance from everyone.

The house phone rang by the kitchen door. *When did that get plugged in?*

It'd better not be another bloke ringing for Monet or he was going to rip the phone off the wall.

'Yeah?' He still wasn't in the mood for niceties.

'Oh, darling, finally.'

'Mum?'

'I've been so worried about you. Sherice and I have been trying to ring you.'

'I've had the phone off the hook because I don't want to talk to Sherice.' Why did he bother answering the bloody phone?

'Sherice is so worried, I tell you. As am I.'

'I'm fine, finishing up the last of the cyclone lock

down around the shed.' He stared out at his new shed. The money he would've spent on an engagement ring paid for the new roof. He still had money in the bank from the last muster, set aside for the wedding that never happened. A ceremony that would have cost him twenty thousand dollars—even with her rich daddy's contribution to the nuptials.

He liked his shed better.

'You should drive to Katherine.'

'No way.' He wasn't going near that town again. He did not want to cross paths with Sherice.

'Well then, catch a plane and come here.'

'Not now, I'm not. Not with this storm.'

'But you have that crazy girl out there.'

'Monet. Her name is, and has always been, Monet, Mum.'

'She's crazy, I tell you. As crazy as her mother, infecting everyone with their madness.'

Tim frowned at the phone. Monet was being a genuine friend, who had always been there for him, even when he had tried to push her away. 'You should be happy I've got a mate out here to help me.'

'Call one of your other friends. Alex? He's a good sort.'

'What have you got against Monet?'

'Um… She's a-a-a bush pilot—'

'Are you being sexist?' His mother hated feminism, preferring her life as the 50s cook-at-home kinda gal. 'Mum, you would be impressed at how clean the place is, and the amount of food Monet's made for me.'

'Sherice told me that Monet had moved right on in, taking over everything.'

Well, the woman was driving his ute like she owned it, and she'd taken over his office and kitchen. But why complain, when his books were getting done and his belly was full. 'Monet is doing what I'm paying her for.'

'Like a hooker. Sherice was telling me Monet's been with all of those stockmen, her reputation is atrocious.'

That burned with stinging licks of anger rising through his chest. 'Mum, I've gotta go.'

'It's Christmas Eve.'

'Yeah, and I've got a lot of stuff to do. I'll call you tomorrow. Merry Christmas.' He hung up the phone, then pulled the chord.

Delivered by the pocket rocket, his mail rested on the side bench. Besides a handful of bills, there were a few Christmas cards. They were the only decorations he had in the place.

He looked around the house, big and empty of furniture. It was still home. But it didn't even feel like Christmas at home.

For as long as he could remember, while people celebrated Halloween, Tim had been made to haul boxes down from the attic just so his mother could start planning Christmas.

His mother started decorating in November, so that

by the time Christmas arrived, Tim was over it.

Over the flashy tinsel.

Over the fake tree that took up half the lounge area, blocking off the TV.

Then there were the decorations he had to duck to miss in the hallway. They weren't allowed to use the special towels in the bathroom or step on the Christmas mats by the doors. There were Christmas tablecloths, couch covers, even aprons and pot holders. All these Christmassy things his mother added to every single year.

Now, there was nothing to show it was the festive season at all. Just baked goods Monet had cooked so his eggs didn't go to waste, and food she'd brought in or foraged in his yard.

Tim peeked inside the fridge.

The tofu had disappeared.

What did she cook with that? Did he eat it?

He spied a granular porridge thing she called *keenwa* and a pudding of chia seeds made with coconut or something. It was different, that's for sure.

Tim doubted Monet knew the name of her dishes either. She'd start with a recipe, and like everything else in her life, she'd wing it and go off in her own direction.

Thankfully, her food was always edible.

Scoffing down a chunk of tasty banana bread she'd loaded with butter and a hint of coconut, Tim headed for the shed. He'd been welding the lock for the door to brace it against the winds.

The storm was coming.

It had finally been upgraded into the cyclone category system.

With a category one cyclone you'd expect a bit of wind and rain. That didn't bother Tim too much, they had tropical storm fronts stronger than that.

With a category two cyclone, you didn't even raise eyebrows over it. But you did gaze over your cyclone kit in case the huffing-puffing wannabe hurricane got up some steam.

When it hit category three, it had warranted enough attention to do a scout around the yard to minimise debris, which they'd done a few days ago while still under a cyclone watch.

But this beast had bounced off the cyclone watch and slid straight into a category four. That's when you dragged out your survival kits and kicked all those storm strategies up a notch, because the mother had turned into a land-hungry typhoon.

If and when they did call out a category five, you started praying as you moved into top gear, deciding whether to stay, or run for the hills.

And this incoming sucker had now hit full-tilt cat-screaming-five.

It had the news hollering that it was a severe tropical cyclone—and they called it freaking Emma!

Over 100 kilometres wide, the cyclone's eye stretched to 25 kilometres, with wind speeds reaching 350 kilometres an hour. She was a gutsy beast with wind gusts ripping up the countryside at a whopping 400 kilometres an hour, while travelling slower than the walking speed of man.

It had Tim's attention.

It's what had him bounding out of bed before daybreak, to fine-tune his cyclone plan.

In his new shed, he welded the last of the locking mechanisms for both doors. All machinery was parked inside or tied down in shelters.

The horses had been set free, letting their natural instincts take care of them. Just like the couple of tawny frogmouth owls who'd been moving swiftly in the daytime, gathering goods for their nest wedged deep in the fork of the tree by the kitchen window. It had three chicks Tim had been watching grow for weeks. They were almost ready to fly—if they survived this storm.

Tim serviced his small fishing boat that was hooked to the back of his ute. His prize air boat was primed and ready to go too. Monet's plane was strapped down tight with his old truck tarp, to protect it from flying debris.

He sharpened his chainsaw and loaded it into his ute, along with assorted oils, fuels, rope, and chains in preparation for clearing roads from the expected tree damage.

ETA for this monstrous storm… midnight.

Merry freaking Christmas.

At the industrial sinks, Tim washed his hands free from oil and dirt, while staring out at the expansive view of his property. No kites glided lazily overhead on the thermals like normal. No cattle or wallabies were about. No birds called to each other. Even the ants had scampered for higher ground.

It was eerily quiet with thick dark grey clouds, moving fast. Not floating. They were hiking it like they were being chased.

Monet's music carried on the wind as he sniffed the air. It was cooling against the humidity that was still thick and muggy. When he copped a whiff of wet paint. He frowned, searching for the source of the aroma. What was Monet painting? And with what?

He stalked around the shed; the smell of fresh paint was undeniable.

He walked backwards toward the house and the main track, looking back at his shed's roof. It was the same shiny new roof.

He then strode around to the other side where the paint fumes were the strongest.

'Oh, hell no.' He scowled up at the roof. 'MONET!' His voice echoed in the valley.

He stormed back to the house. 'MONET!'

Of course, she was ignoring him. Again.

'*Bandit.*' He whistled and in a few seconds his dog came flying from around the back of the house.

'Good dog,' he said, patting the eager canine. 'Where is she?' He headed toward the rear of his home. 'You know, I own you, right? You're my dog,' he said to the blue cattle dog that raced ahead to where the music got louder.

'That'd be bloody right.' Tim stood on the edge of his clipped lawn that had been excruciating to listen to, but now looked good.

And on that neat lawn was Monet, lying in the old bathtub with a tonne of bubbles. She had a flash cocktail glass in one hand, a plateful of snacks and her stereo stood on an old crate nearby. With her head resting back on a towel, she sang to the music.

She looked pretty damned comfortable.

'OI!'

Monet raised her sunglasses to peek at him, turning down her stereo that went everywhere with her.

How something that small could be so loud was a technological mystery to him.

'Oh, you're still here.'

'I live here. Remember? My station.'

'So says the Posh Prince. Are you going to fire me with that death look? Oh, wait, you're always wearing that look. So, what did I do wrong now?'

He scowled at her, pointing back to his shed. 'What the hell did you do to my shed.'

'What shed? This is a station with lots of sheds,' she said, sipping from her cocktail adorned with an umbrella and a chunk of pineapple.

Was that a chunk of their peace pineapple?

It didn't matter now because their truce was well and truly over.

'You know which one.' He pointed to his new shed, approaching the temptress in the tub with her tiny pink-painted toenails poking out of the bubbles. 'You tagged my shed. I can't believe you're the roof painter terrorising Elsie Creek.'

'Terrorising.' She laughed, reaching over to turn up her music.

'Nope.' He swiped her phone and speaker, he wasn't done yet. 'What on earth possessed you to paint my roof? ON. MY. NEW. SHED.'

'Touchy.'

'Since when can you paint, Claude? You have no artistic flair. You failed art in school by doing stick figures. How on earth did you do that roof? Why?'

'It needed a little something. I like it.'

'It's not your shed.'

'I know. You can't see it when you drive in.'

'How long has it been up there? You've only…' Then he realised. 'You've been sneaking out while I've been in bed, sick.'

'I don't sneak.'

'I heard the screen door open and close, wondering what you're doing.' And why the house was quiet for so damned long.

'You could have asked.'

'I'm asking now. Why did you paint my roof?'

'Do you know what it is?'

'It's paint.' He barked at her. 'On a new roof. My

roof.'

'Fine, I'll go and strip it all off if you're that upset over it.'

'Damned straight I am.'

But then she stood up. Naked.

Bubbles slid off her beautifully bare body. He forgot what they were talking about. Arguing... *Um, what?*

He took in her stance, the weight on one hip, arms crossed, with her chin jutted out. She was trouble. Big trouble in a compact package. Except the curve of her lips suggested she was more amused than angry. While the rest of her was a slippery slide of bubbles revealing more luscious skin.

'Okay, we're done here.' She gave him an annoyed toss of her mop of hair. It was her middle finger look he knew so well. She'd done it to others in her past, present, and whatever dared to stand in the way of her future.

But his eyes kept taking a slow tour of her body, lingering on all her good bits. His nostrils flared as he clenched his hands into fists that itched to touch her.

Then she wrapped her package in a towel.

But it was Christmas Eve. Why couldn't he unwrap his gift now?

'I'll strip your roof, then I'll pack and leave, because you're back to normal. Not that I like this normal. But hey, I've finished your books and house, so my contract commitments are all completed. You don't need a farm-sitter, and I'm sick of playing your babysitter.'

Crossing arms over his chest, he glowered at her.

'I miss the old Tim. If you see that Tim, ask him if he can come back and say g'day some time,' she said, walking away in a towel.

'What do you mean by that?'

She stopped and faced him.

Unable to help himself, he leaned closer to peek at her cleavage.

'The Tim who used to be fun and joined in. Remember him?' Her voice was loaded with sympathy. The same emotion that showed in her eyes, bottomless and compassionate.

He could sink into them for decades.

'Where's the Tim who didn't wait for an invitation to join in on the fun?'

He'd wanted to join in, but he'd been too sick—and was a stubborn fool. But his shed!

'You used to be the one in charge of the fun, remember? You were the one who loved music. Buying all this music in my name and collecting it from the Inn, because your mother checked your mail and hid stuff from you.' She pointed at him, saying, 'It was you who invented the game of roof sitting on the Inn at night before you went to boarding school. It was you who led those sneaky midnight sessions to shift Nasty Nancy's gnomes around and all those other games on the midnight streets of Elsie Creek.' She stepped back with pain wrinkling her brow. Pain that carried through to her voice. 'You're not the Tim

I've loved since the day we met. Where's that guy? The fun guy who was my champion in school, sticking up for me when kids picked on me about my mother?'

His heart went cold. He almost shivered under the outback summer sunset, feeling her hurt. Had she overheard him talking to his mother?

'Because…' She stepped so close he could smell the delicate floral fragrance from the bubbles still coating her supple skin, but the soul in her eyes was vintage. She poked his chest lightly, yet it stabbed through his heart like a thousand swords. 'You've turned into this whiny boy who sounds just like his mother.'

'Oi.' He did not whine like his mother.

'Sorry, I thought you'd like the roof. I bet your dad would have loved it. But, I guess, I've lost that best friend because this guy,' she said, waving her hand over him like she was telling a waiter to take away some foul dish, 'I don't know this Tim, and I don't want to.' She turned and swaggered away.

Tim dropped clumsily onto the edge of the old bathtub made into a garden ornament filled with bubbles. He exhaled with heavy shoulders folding under the humid air, watching Monet disappear around the corner.

His dog lay nearby, giving him a whimpering look.

'Do you think I'm whiny, too?'

Bandit thumped his tail, then bolted to the house, leaving Tim to sit alone, hearing the kitchen door close.

He scooped up the cocktail glass Monet had left

behind. 'Mmm, not bad.' It had a coconut mango flavour.

That's when he noticed his mango trees had been stripped bare.

Monet always did make wicked cocktails. It was her Sunday game, to sit back in her kiddie pool stored at the Unofficial Elsie Creek Inn. She'd drag it out to the patchy lawn under the shade of the massive tree in the back yard to look over the horse paddocks. There, with whoever dared to join her, she would sip on nameless cocktails, making up names for clouds while cooking her Sunday roast on the barbecue. She never flew on Sundays, calling it her day as a minimalist to do the barest minimum.

Tim was tempted to sit in the bath and stare at the spectacular view she had from the tub. The sunset stretched its red and golden rays through the clouds, across his property. A scene he hadn't bothered to look at in months.

He frowned at his shed.

The frown faltered as he tilted his head.

Lord love her, she was the most irritating creature on the planet.

His new roof, though?

He wiped over his face, then poked up the brim of his hat and sipped on the cocktail with the pink umbrella in it. Sucking it dry, he then ate the chunks of their peace pineapple.

When did he learn to hate his best friend?

All he'd done since Monet had arrived was argue with her, trying to push her away.

In return, she'd given him a gift—not the roof—but her friendship. She'd done so much for him over the years and this is how he treated her?

Tim narrowed his eyes at his shed's roof like he was in a museum. She'd painted a big bloody Brahman. It was a good one, in a proud show stance, wearing a prized competition blue sash just like the ones he had lined up along the office wall. The words inside the ribbon covering the cow on his shed's roof said, *'Rigby Downs, blue ribbon cattle country.'*

She was right, his dad would have loved it.

Monet stormed out the front door in her cargo pants and boots and stropped across the yard.

Away from him.

Was it too late? Had the damage been done?

His heart dropped and he raced after her. 'Monet?'

NINE

Monet tied a bandana over her wet hair, then slid the long-sleeved shirt on over her singlet. Tightening her rock-climbing harness, she hoisted her ropes higher along her shoulder. Ready to paint.

She was this close to punching something or crying. But Monet never wasted her time on tears. So why did she let this guy get to her?

'Monet?' Tim jogged over to meet her, carrying her empty cocktail glass.

'Did you drink my drink on me?'

'Yeah, it was good too,' he said with a cheesy grin. 'Have you got any more?'

'I'm—' She pointed to his roof.

'Leave it. I like it. You could have said something.'

'And miss the whole shouting fireworks? Are you kidding?'

'Okay, I'm sorry.' He said it with a palm over his heart and lowered brow. His light blue eyes shot straight to her soul and her knees weakened.

Nope. Not giving in. So she jutted out her chin, with a hand on her hip. 'For what?'

'For shouting at you. But it ticked me off that you'd done it without asking me.'

'I did it as a surprise.'

'I get that now. Hey, since when can you paint?'

She shrugged. 'It's paint by numbers.'

'And numbers you do well, as my creative little bookkeeper. So, Claude, how?' Tim pointed to his shed roof. They couldn't see her artwork from this side.

Monet had always wanted to paint, and being named after one of the greatest impressionists of all time, she was ashamed she couldn't even draw stick figures properly. 'It's a program. I take the measurements of the roof, pick a picture and then it maps it out for me on a graph with numbers for paint colour.'

'And we know you read maps well.'

'Duh, pilot.'

'Did you smuggle in the paint too?'

Was he sucking up? 'Spray paint, it's easy to carry while climbing.'

'Don't leave.'

'Excuse me?' Her heart flip-flopped at the sincerity of his words.

'I don't want you flying in this storm.'

Yeah, right, for her safety, nothing more. 'I'll be fine.'

'No. You're staying, look at it.' Tim pointed to the storm front on the eastern horizon. It was thick, black and had monstrous angry clouds rolling like a slow-moving airborne tsunami.

They both knew it was coming.

The wind picked up, tousling her hair as she checked the area for crosswinds. If she pushed it, there might still be enough time to make it back to town.

But then she'd have to deal with Mickey as they battled the weather to tie down Gertrude, who was safely tucked away now. 'I'll leave in the morning, then.'

He nodded.

Deal done.

She plucked her cocktail glass from his big hand and headed back to the house. 'Can I get my speaker back?'

'If you'll make me one of those drinks?'

'Oh, really?' She peeked at him over her shoulder, dumping her rock-climbing kit by the verandah's steps.

'It is Christmas Eve, you know.'

'Is it? I forgot.' Two more sleeps and the whole sucky-Santa story would be all over for another year. 'Huh, my contractual commitments truly end tomorrow.'

Tim grabbed her arm, pulling her to a standstill by the front door. 'I'm still here, Monet, it's just that...' He looked away, as if ashamed of himself.

Her heart squeezed to see him so vulnerable like this. 'Sherice really did a number on you, huh?'

He frowned hard at the concrete.

That cow! 'We could blow up her picture and throw darts at it, while you tell me all about it?'

'Would you listen?'

'When have I ever *not* listened to you?'

He sighed, sliding his hands into his denim pockets. 'You know,' he said, with the frown disappearing as he looked back over the station, 'I wanted this to be my first Christmas to start my own family tradition, free from all of Mum's stuff. That last Christmas, Dad and I were looking for excuses to avoid the house, to not get roped into hanging any more trinkets.'

His confession melted her on the spot. She was tempted to ruffle his hair and say, *there, there, honey, it'll all be right in the morning.* 'What were you planning to do? Because you know I don't do Christmas.'

'You've got your candy cane stash that you won't share.'

'Hey, that's the only thing I like about Christmas. As much as I love you, no one touches my candy canes but me.'

'I know. Remember, I used to buy you boxes of them.'

And that stopped like everything else. 'Okay...' It took everything inside her to not pull the face of horrors, when she asked, 'What do you want to do for Christmas?'

'I dunno?' He shrugged. 'Drink beer.'

'Boring. It's time to flip that playlist, babe, because you've been drinking beer and watching cricket for how long?'

He scratched the back of his head as the wind picked up and the rain started to fall lightly. Lightning flashed in the distance, followed by an earthy rumble of thunder she felt through her boots.

'I'll make cocktails and you can choose the music?'

'Me? I—ah…' He rubbed at his eyebrow, holding out her blue-tooth speaker as if the technology was too much.

'Just pick a playlist, they're named after moods or themes. It's also your turn to cook. So why not dazzle me with your barbecue skills?'

He nodded, with his grin creeping back. 'I do have some decent steak inside, but what about decorations?' Tim asked, opening the front door for her.

He had always been a gentleman like that. Was the real Tim making a comeback?

'Decorations?' She looked around the empty house. She didn't do decorations, not when she'd spent the last twenty years avoiding Christmas. 'I'll get the candles everyone gave me for Christmas.'

'We'll need them, for when we lose power.' They both looked through the window to the fast-approaching storm.

'I'll tape up the windows while I have a think about it.'

'I'll do the barbie. Do we need salads?'

'They're already in the fridge.' She grinned at his hesitant step while he glanced at the fridge. 'Yes, my love, you've been eating tofu and quinoa.'

Tim made a gagging face as he headed out the kitchen door. Monet went in the opposite direction to empty and drag away her bubble bath.

In the office she created a big X made from strips of masking tape on all the large windows. She then wrote *Merry Xmas* backwards in marker pen on the glass. It looked crappy, but it made Tim smile, so it was worth the effort.

'My mother would have a fit at that,' he said, pointing to her pathetic scribblings.

'I'm not a calligrapher—I've got it! Let's do everything your mother would have hated for Christmas decorations.'

'Sorry?'

'You know, no order, completely chaotic, handmade whatever, mish-mash, slap-happy stuff we come up with. What matters the most is that we bothered to make an effort.' She pointed to the *Xmas* scribbled on his window and drew a fat stick figure beside it. 'Don't stress, this isn't permanent.'

'What is that?'

'Santa.' She cocked her head at it and screwed up her nose. 'Pretend a kid drew it.'

'You can paint roofs but not a window?'

'I'm trying.' She shrugged, handing him a stack of markers. 'You can draw whatever you want, I'll just do the words for outside decorations.'

The guy needed it and hopefully this would bring him back. It broke her heart to see him suffering.

She missed the Tim she'd always adored. This new Tim hadn't been any fun to hang out with at all, and with the cyclone bearing down on them, they both needed a distraction.

Just for Tim, she could paste on a fake smile and pretend she was into the whole ho-ho-ho hurlathon, because underneath she really loved the guy.

She'd always loved Tim. She was just never good enough for him.

TEN

Outside the storm grew stronger. Inside, Tim and Monet sat at the kitchen table, covered in assorted tools and cocktail glasses, jugs and alcoholic mixers. They cut stars with tinsnips out of old beer cans, wearing paper crowns made from stapled printer paper they'd raided from the office supplies. It was their attempt at making hats resembling the paper crowns found in Christmas bonbons.

'Shane Warne,' Tim said, removing his paper crown to read the name Monet had scrawled on as part of their drinking game.

'Finally,' said Monet, with the names Mae West and Harley Quinn scribbled on her own crown. 'I thought you would've worked it out before this, especially after your days of beer-bingeing snooze-fests in front of the cricket.'

'But it came in handy.' Tim cut out another star then punched a hole in the tip for Monet to lace his fishing line through.

'They're brilliant,' she said, twirling a tin star that caught the kitchen's light.

Tim hadn't done this sort of stuff since he was a barefoot kid lapping up the adventures of his childhood at the Unofficial Elsie Creek Inn. Monet's grandma would have them making stuff from scrap to take home for the holidays, painting eggs for Easter, or creating cards for Christmas.

'We need some sort of a tree,' Monet said, placing the stars near the paper chains they'd stapled together.

It looked like crap. But it killed time while the storm barrelled down upon them.

'I've seen some pretty stylish coils of barbed wire made into Christmas trees that guard those dressed-up outback gnomes.'

'Yeah, well my barbed wire is in the shed. Tell me you're not thinking about dressing up an ant mound in this weather?' Tim faced the depths of blackness beyond his back door. Every few seconds and in all directions, the lightning lit up the sky like muzzle-flash bombs. It had been raining heavily for a few hours now, but the music, cocktails and craft lessons had kept them busy.

Something banged hard against the side of the house. He had to see.

He opened his back door to a howling gale. Trees were being whipped around like feathers with their leaves stuck to windows under the relentless sheet of powering rain. Another loud bang made him flinch as something hit the other side of the house, but the place stood solid.

Debris, branches, leaves and rain pelted past him. He reached out and caught the first treetop that rolled past. It was nothing more than a common scraggly gum. He shook off the excess water, then used brute force just to push his back door shut.

'How's this?' Tim held up his prize like a dripping, limp fish freshly pulled from the stormy seas. It was scrappy and crappy—but the way her eyes and smile lit up you'd think he'd snagged a record-winning, prize-fighting, barramundi.

'Perfect. We just need a base.' From the front doorway, Monet dragged a dead pot plant into the middle of his lounge room.

Tim smiled with a warmth growing from inside his chest at the little lady doing everything his mum would have hated. There was no time wasted on positioning it for that perfect aha effect. It was slap-happy *look at what we did!*

Considering how much she loathed this time of year, the effort Monet was putting into Christmas for him was incredible. The pocket rocket was on the job, pinching an old Hawaiian shirt from his cupboard and wrapping it around the pot plant to create a base for the tree.

Tim staked the limp eucalyptus branch into the pot

like he was planting the American flag on the moon. They then covered it with their handmade stars, which shifted with the whirling ceiling fans.

Standing back, he screwed his nose up at the flimsy monstrosity. What were they thinking?

Monet tossed the paper chain around the base and with hands on her hips, stood beside him. 'It doesn't have to be pretty or perfect to be beautiful. It just has to be real and have meaning for us.'

Didn't that hit him like a bolt to the heart.

It was a simple tree, not even a tree, but they'd made it work as a momentary reprieve from the storm pounding against the windows.

The television played scenes of his favourite Christmas movie, *Die Hard*. His mother loathed that movie, which made the memory all the more precious. It was part of Tim's annual ritual with his dad, to sneak over to the shed with the spare television to hide from his mother and her Christmas preparations.

Now, the movie played on mute in all its *Yippee-Ki-Yay* gloriousness on the wide screen.

Monet's music, which wasn't Christmassy at all, played in the background.

No bells. Monet had put her foot down on the bells. She hated bells, even though she'd drawn some on the windows.

They had a fridge full of food, their bellies were stuffed from his barbecued steak, and there was a load of other treats to pick at all night. They also had music, cocktails, and now they had a tree and decorations.

Is this what Christmas was all about? 'We're missing something?'

Monet stood with hands on hips, squinting at the scene. Her beautiful brain, designed for mischief, was no doubt working overtime. 'Pictures.'

'What?'

'Pictures. Those perfectly prepared happy snaps people put on their cards or calendars?' Her grin grew as her eyes sparkled. 'I knew this guy who'd give me one every year then tell me to burn it.'

'Ugh.' He groaned, face-palming himself. Tim's mother had forced Tim and his dad to pose for Christmas cards she'd send out mid-November. 'Don't make me wear a jumper. Or a tie. Or a shirt.'

Monet laughed.

Finally, she was laughing with him. It was a sweet sound. It magnified the warmth he'd felt in his chest earlier to punch-drunk teenage giddiness. His jaw ached smiling with her. What was going on? He'd never reacted like this with anyone.

'No. You can go shirtless and wear your hat indoors. Not your good town hat either. Wear your sweaty, everyday, working hat, we'll decorate it with beer stars instead of the swagman corks.' She pushed him into place, like a model of sorts, next to his crappy tree.

'Can we freeze the movie at the messiest part?'

'Splendid idea.' She handed him the TV's remote while she scooped up their over-garnished cocktail glasses, and her phone with its long selfie wand. 'Bandit, you're included.'

'We can never show this to Mum.'

'Why not?'

'There's a dog in the house.'

'It's your house,' she said, rolling those incredible eyes at him.

'Oh, you finally remembered that, did you? My house, huh? I swear it's been overrun by the pocket rocket bush pilot,' he mumbled as they jostled for position.

The dog sat at their feet, wearing one of their paper crowns. Tim and Monet raised their cocktail glasses decorated with chunks of fruit and umbrellas. He was shirtless, in his Akubra, board shorts, and bare feet that showed off his sock tan. 'If I had a bow tie, I'd wear it.'

'I'll send you one for next Christmas.' Monet wore her shorts and singlet, sliding on her aviators for that effortless cool look.

They posed.

Click.

As his eyes adjusted from the phone's camera flash, he peeked over her shoulder, admiring her soft, fruity aroma. 'It's too straight and serious. It needs to be messier.' Those Christmas photos were awkward, stiff and serious sessions while overdressed.

'I'm in for messier,' said his impish offsider.

And for the next ten minutes they pulled faces and poses around the treetop he'd caught in the wind, wearing stars they'd cut out of beer cans.

Tim helped her choose the best of their worst images and she loaded them onto her Instagram feed. Monet was popular, with loads of followers, including some he knew.

He scrolled through all the other images of his friends with their families. He almost forgot his own drama, pausing at his own image wearing an enormous smile, with Monet by his side and the dog joining in.

Tim took a step back.

He looked happy and they'd been having a ball. Even though they were on the edge of the fast-approaching cyclone's furious eyewall. And that's where most of the damage was done. If they got through that and hit the eye, they'd handle the rest.

He looked up from the phone's screen to spot Monet shifting a load of cushions down the corridor.

'What are you doing?' Tim asked, following her into the bathroom.

'Just in case,' she replied, dumping them into his king-sized bathtub.

'Have you tried out my new tub yet?'

'No. I like the old one. It's got a better view.' She tapped his shoulder, giving him a cheeky grin and headed back to grab more.

In the bathroom he discovered his PC's hard drive was wrapped in thick plastic. It sat alongside his personal records in plastic boxes tied to the towel rack. 'You've been busy.'

'It's my job,' Monet said, returning with candles, food and drinking water.

Well, he was paying her to do the books and house-sit the place. 'I've um…'

'Grab the photos, trophies and ribbons from your room. I've got a spare plastic box for them. I've already packed your blue ribbons and trophies from the office and lounge.'

Monet had turned his bathroom into a cyclone shelter. It would happen eventually. It was that, or they'd both get drunk and sleep through it, because the wind was now howling. With each gust it threw sideways rain over the house in a blanket of water like violent waves pounding a ship at sea.

Back at the kitchen table, Monet pushed her empty glass in front of him while scrolling through her tablet. 'It's your turn to make the cocktails. There's plenty of ingredients to create your own unique flavour.'

'Only if you tell me how you ended up being the roof tagger?'

'Don't tell anyone.'

'It'll be kinda hard to hide it after what you've done out there.' Tim pointed to his graffitied shed, hidden by the solid wall of sideways rain. 'It won't take long for people to work it out.'

'I'm surprised I've gotten away with it this long.

Although, I think I stuffed up doing the cop shop. Marcus is spewing.'

'Marcus, huh?' Tim hid his frown, draining the last of his drink. 'So, where did you get the idea to paint roofs?'

'I used to play solitaire all the time, waiting for passengers or freight to show up at the airstrips. One day, while sick of playing cards, I remembered I had a spare can of spray paint. It was left over from Mickey trying to teach me to do night landings.'

'Night landings?'

'Yeah, I've got no problem flying at night, trusting my screens. But with night landings, not knowing what the runway condition is like, I can't do it. So, Mickey would light up the strip and spray paint this glow in the dark X at the start of the runway for me and I'd aim for that.'

'Can you land now?'

'At night? Without an X? No. I try to avoid it if I can. Dusk is as late as I'll fly.'

Tim poured vodka and white rum into their jug, creating some cocktail concoction from the recipe on her tablet. 'Am I doing this right?'

'It's a splash of this and a dash of that, then mix and taste.' They splashed several spirits over crushed ice, then threw in assorted chunks of chopped tropical fruit.

Tim stirred the contents in the jug, poured, then tasted it. 'It's drinkable.'

'And that's all that matters, my love.' Monet sipped from her cocktail glass crowded with fruit, a green cocktail umbrella, a blue flamingo swivel stick and a metal straw that she used as a fruit skewer. 'This is really nice.'

He took a deep swig, patting his bare chest as the smooth cool drink satisfied his taste buds. 'Yep, I might quit farming and start my own cocktail lounge. What do you reckon?'

'We'll need lights, bar fridges, and a blender. I'll get you a flashy bow tie, but the shirt is optional. We'll sell more tickets by the hour if you remain topless, babe.'

He chuckled and sipped his drink, getting a good buzz out of it. 'So, you became the roof painter because you got bored waiting at airstrips? How? When layovers, passenger and freight delays are part of your job.' It's why she had a loaded tablet of not only music, but books to read while waiting.

But for Claude to paint roofs—when she couldn't even do stick figures properly—it was hard to believe. 'Tell me you stole some of Santa's elves to do the job for you.'

She shook her soft mop at him. 'No one has ever noticed, and I've been doing it for ages. I used to paint the runway's dirt that blew away in a few days. Then I graduated to the small lean-tos you find on most station airstrips. I've even tagged airport sheds in lots of remote towns and mine sites. They were only simple images that suited that place.' She fidgeted with her cocktail straw and said in a quieter voice, 'I can only do retro-styled cartoon images, nothing too arty. Although the program I use calls it poster-styled pop art. Kitschy stuff.'

'Oh, really?' He arched his eyebrow at her. 'Did you tap into your inner ironic Monet, Claude?'

She shared a nervous laugh.

'My station hands told me the Mad Hatter on the Elsie Creek Tea House is a must-see.'

'The town's traditional tea house is a museum now.'

'Huh?' He'd missed out on so much, because Monet used to keep him up to date with weekly phone calls and regular visits. 'Why did you stop visiting? Calling?' Being his friend.

'You asked me to.'

He frowned, shuffling in his seat. 'No, I didn't.'

'Oh yes, you did. You, your mother and your ex.'

'When?'

'At your father's funeral.'

He dropped his head, scrubbing his face as the memory of that horrific day returned. 'I didn't know about—'

'Your mother and your ex?'

'No. I mean, yes, but…' Tim sighed, staring into his drink. That day had been horrible, burying his father. He'd done his best to stand tall. He had to. With his mother on one side, Sherice on the other, they'd trapped him.

Tim had lost the father he respected, the man who'd always been there to share the burden. There was no more Dad to give straight answers to Tim's questions. Instead, he'd been left with two sobbing women wetting the shirt and tie he only wore at weddings and funerals.

That day, he'd been made to face the town. A sea of people, shaking his hand; accepting their condolences until they all rolled into one long blur.

Only one face had caught his attention, wiping away her tears at the back of the crowd.

And Monet never cried for anyone.

Tim hadn't been able to get near her and she'd done her best to avoid him. But when she made a move to go out to the back of the pub, he needed air and followed. Right by the back door, she'd looked up at him with red eyes as raw as he felt on the inside. Neither of them had said a word.

He'd hugged her. Or she'd hugged him. It didn't matter. But they'd just stood there, never saying a damned word.

Monet had comforted him when he'd needed it the most, both holding onto each other in silence.

But didn't that screw up everything—because that's when the fireworks started.

ELEVEN

'I only hugged you, just like I've always done,' Monet said, seated opposite Tim at the kitchen table filled with cocktail ingredients and tools. On that day, the guy needed a hug. It was a purely innocent moment of shared grief. After all, he'd just buried the father he adored.

'But they didn't like it,' she said. *They* being Tim's mother and Sherice, who shrieked like a pair of tone-deaf banshees out the back of the pub.

'You walked away,' Tim said with a frown.

'So I didn't cause a scene at your father's wake. I walked away out of respect for you and your dad. But those two women had already made up their minds we were doing something wrong—which we weren't. You know I don't sleep with my friends.'

'I told them we're mates.'

'They didn't believe you. Especially when your mother cornered me in the pub's hallway a few minutes later, telling me I was no longer welcome at Rigby Downs.' Sitting up with square shoulders, the heat of hate churned inside at the memory. 'If I ever showed my face out here again, the charming and sweet Mrs Beryl Kirby would have had me charged for trespassing. Beryl swore she'd charge me with it too; as the widow she owned the station.'

He sat straighter, blinking. 'No, she doesn't.'

She knew that, but she wasn't going to argue with the widow at her husband's funeral. So Monet walked away. Well, she tried to… 'Oh, and then your sweet *sugar*, Sherice, tried to bitch-slap me in the pub's toilets, accusing me of taking you away from her. And then you…' She sat back in her chair, cradling her over-crowded cocktail glass in her lap with her anger simmering under the surface. 'I adored your father and I was only there to pay my respects. But when you asked me to leave…' It broke her heart. Obliterating it.

You'd think, after suffering through the many layers of heartbreak in her life, Tim had somehow pierced her heart of stone, which she'd always considered impenetrable. Yet that prick had sliced and diced it with icy-cold steel swords, destroying what was left of her soul.

'I didn't mean for you to leave everything,' Tim said in a gravelly tone.

'You said go, so I did,' she snarled. 'Why hang around when I'm not wanted?' It was a lesson well-learned as a kid. She'd lost count of the many times she'd been told to go away by those parents who didn't want the crazy woman's kid infecting their children with her madness.

'I didn't want that.'

'Well, you could've called. You could've emailed me. But no, it was complete radio silence,' she said bitterly. 'Then out of the blue I get this cold email requesting that I house-sit your place for Christmas with a very specific list of tasks in a contract. We'd never needed a contract before in all the years I've farm-sat this place.' It had ticked her right off.

The only reason Monet had accepted the contract's terms was because she wanted to be alone to escape the silly season; and yet, here they were.

'Did you send me that contract, or was it all sweet 'n sugary Sherice?' The unveiled bitterness dripped from her words.

Tim winced at the name, taking a deep drink from his cocktail glass.

Technically, he was supposed to be on his extended honeymoon. *Bugger!* No wonder he'd been so miserable.

'I ah…' He rubbed his eyes. 'She was there.'

'Typing or watching word for word over your shoulder.'

He shrugged.

'Man, they had you under their thumb.' She pointed

her drink at him. 'I warned you about that. Yet you accuse me of taking over, but I don't. I just do what I'm contracted to do, as quickly as possible, so I can then do the fun stuff. But I know Beryl and Sherice sucked you right into their web while you were grieving for your dad. I saw it happening at the funeral, you looked like you were suffocating.'

The poor guy didn't look too crash hot right now either.

She hated upsetting the guy, forcing herself to take a deep breath to push her anger down into her belly. 'Look, all I was trying to do was give you some space to breathe and to let you know that I had your back. That's why they didn't want me around, they would've lost control of the Posh Prince.'

Instead, Monet was the one who'd lost more than her best friend. On that fine foul day, she'd lost all forms of hope. Why bother to hope for anything when it only bites you on the back, leaving deep, jagged scars that never heal.

The wind swallowed the music with its never-ending scream that made the windows rattle. They had opened the windows a little to stop the pressure, or they'd explode, and that would test out her masking tape X's.

Forgetting the storm, she admired Tim's silhouette with his shiny eyes. A hint of a smile grew as he stared at his simple tree in the lounge.

His mother would have hated it, which, of course, made Monet love it even more.

She could picture Mrs Beryl Kirby's face, twisted in disgust at Tim sitting at the table in shorts, no shirt, and in bare feet. The coveted kitchen table was covered in tools, beer tins and cocktail mixes, with the working dog, Bandit, asleep under the table.

'I like the tree. It's growing on me,' Tim said.

'Me too. It's pretty stylish. Your dad would've liked it… I miss Mr Kirby. He even liked my stick figures and would mess up my hair and say, *good job for trying.* Unlike your mother, who hates me for breathing.'

He spun around to face her. 'Why?'

Damn. Why did she open her mouth?

'Go on, tell me why my mother hates you so much?'

She sat straighter with chin raised. If he really had to know… 'My mother told me why.'

'Where is your mum?'

'In Spain. Oh, I must send those images to Marcus of how sexy the Spanish Police look in their uniforms. Better yet, I should send him one—the women in Elsie Creek would thank me for it.'

'Marcus, huh?' Tim frowned, slopping more cocktail mix into their glasses. 'How is your mother?'

Wow. The Posh Prince dared to ask. 'Great. She's remarried to this amazing guy. Living on this farm set in the hills, making jam and other preserves from her olive grove. It's a beautiful countryside.'

'She's okay though?'

'Her bipolar, you mean?'

'Yeah.'

'As long as she's on her meds, Mum is fine. Her new husband knows her triggers and that man adores her; he treats her like a queen.'

'When did you go to Spain?'

'Last year for a bit.'

'She won't visit?'

'This place? Never,' Monet scoffed. 'They were cruel to her.'

'Before or—'

'Anytime and every time.' Monet shuffled in her seat, staring at her cocktail glass. If only they could hear her music to block out her thoughts as a wave of heavy sadness rippled over her. It was like weighty, thick black plastic was pressing on her shoulder blades, forcing her spine to curve under the pressure. Where were her happy tunes when she needed them?

'All right, I'll admit it...' Tim drained his entire cocktail. Slamming down the glass on the table, he dug around inside it with his fork for the fruit. 'I got screwed over by the women in my life. You're excluded, because you were the only one who was right.'

Did she dare sing out *told you so*?

'I was grieving over Dad and got taken advantage of.' He then sighed and said, 'I didn't want to completely cut you out of my life.'

'You couldn't call me without getting into trouble. I get it.' *Chicken.* 'You wanted them to be happy, which would have made you happy.' She patted his forearm, saying, 'As I've said before, I truly did want you to find your happily ever after.'

He grabbed her hand, rubbing his thumb across the back of it, sending tingles up her arm. 'What about your happily ever after?'

'Me? I'm fine.' She pulled her hand back and took a deep swig of her cocktail.

'Why does my mum…' Tim hesitated as if searching for the right word?

'Hate me?'

'I was going to say dislike you?'

He was always the chivalrous diplomat. Always seen as the good guy, while Monet got called trouble. Yet, Tim had another side, rarely shown to anyone else, where he was just as mischievous as her.

That was until Sherice came sashaying along with her bouncy blonde curls, with her hips swinging and that shining smile of sweetness.

'I dare you to ask Mommy Dearest that question. I bet Beryl will answer with the usual about my lack of blue-blood pedigree. Oh, and she'll probably go on about how my screwed-up genetics aren't good enough to be breaking bread with you at this table.' Monet patted the overcrowded tabletop that would have Mrs Beryl Kirby crow like a constipated rooster at daybreak. 'If you really want to know, ask your mother. But I should warn you, the answer will not make you happy. When I found out, it all made sense to me.' Although, it might force Tim to look at his mother in a whole new light—if the mummy's boy dared.

'My mother said they locked your mu—Emma, away.'

'My mother voluntarily booked herself in for treatment,' she said back smartly. Monet had told no one this, not even her BFF, Lucy. So why was she telling Tim now?

They'd always managed to avoid the topic, sharing those comfortable silences she didn't get with anyone else. But he'd been there—he knew. He had never needed to ask about the details. Ever—until today.

Was the storm not only ripping up the countryside, but also dragging up the deep dark junk of their past?

'My grandparents said my mother could come back and take care of me anytime she wanted,' Monet said.

'But she never did—and you used to hate her for that.'

'I didn't know she'd voluntarily checked herself in, because Mum believed she had failed me. Failed my brother.' Her heart turned to sludge that filled prehistoric tar pits, trapping it in an endless depth of sorrow. *This conversation sucked.*

'But you know what?' Monet rested her forearms on the table and wiped at the beads of condensation from her cocktail glass. 'I'd learned that there's this amazing thing, far more powerful than hate—it's called forgiveness.' Maybe she should try it with Beryl, if they ever saw each other again?

'So, you finally forgave your mother?'

'I'll admit it was a tough lesson learned when I went to Spain. We cried. We drank. We danced. And we did an insane amount of olives. I never knew there were so many ways to eat olives. But it was good.' She then raised her glass to Tim. 'As my Christmas present to you, I want to say that I forgive you.'

'For what?'

'For being a princely turd-of-a-friend who dumped me for a bottle blonde in cowboy boots and her puny pretend rodeo belt buckle.'

'You sound jealous.'

'I was. She stole my friend. So now I'm giving you the opportunity to still be friends.'

He squinted at her, giving her a long hard look that had her turning inside out, exposing all of her secrets. Was he going to say no?

'Friends—' He paused, then he grinned and said, 'always. We've been through too much together, not to be.' He held up his glass and they clinked them together.

She was so relieved she wanted to hug him.

But that's when the lights went out.

The front door trembled against the roaring wind of a thousand jet engines. Sideways sheets of rain pelted against the groaning roof. The sudden drop in air pressure pressed against her eardrums, reminding her of the cabin pressure when landing her plane, only stronger.

She squeezed his big hand tight. 'It's here.'

TWELVE

They sat in the king-sized bathtub filled with cushions, Tim by the tap end, Monet opposite. The cocktail jug rested on the floor. Flickering candlelight that had been Monet's Christmas presents she shared, had shadows dancing along the tiled walls.

'If this is your idea of mother nature's playlist, I want to switch the channel,' Monet called out over the wind's howl. Shivering, goose pimples squirrelled along her arms.

Tim rubbed her arms, to warm her and soothe them both.

The noise was horrific. The whining so loud it was like they were inside a turbine engine. Unseen and unknown projectiles slammed against the roof and walls as the rain pelted like stones against the windows. Both of them were waiting for the glass to break.

It was almost midnight, and the small battery fan was trying its best to cool the humid bathroom.

'Party in the smallest room of the house,' said Tim, praying his groaning roof would hold.

'And with no room for bad vibes.' She swallowed a few times, staring at the darkened window as the light of the candles reflected in her worried eyes.

'I'm glad you're here,' he said.

'What?'

'You heard me.'

Her cheeky grin was a giveaway.

He liked that grin. 'Hey, how is it that the shortest person in this place is taking up all the room.'

She lay back like she'd done in the outdoor tub earlier today.

Unable to help himself, he skimmed his hands over her lower legs. 'Smooth.'

'You can massage my feet if you like. Consider it my Chrissy present,' she said, floating one pink-toenailed foot in front of his face.

He caught it, wrapping both of her legs around him and looked down at her cocooned in a bed of plush cushions inside his bathtub. 'Claude?'

'Yes, Your Highness?'

His voice deepened as he eyed every inch of her body. 'If this was our last night on earth…?' He let the question hang in the air and would blame it on the cocktails—but that was tomorrow's problem, when all he saw was the now.

He hoped she could read his mind. This cyclone, the cocktails, and a beautiful woman on her back in his bathtub—the combination was all too potent.

He'd seen her naked. Now he wanted to see all of her again.

Braced and ready for action, he watched her dainty throat flex as she swallowed. Her dirty blonde hair was soft and messy. He wanted to run his fingers through it to drag her in close for a kiss.

Instead, he waited for a sign.

It was all up to Monet now.

Would she break her rules for him?

She curled her soft hand around his jaw and studied his face with eyes that read deep into his soul. Then, ever so slowly, she returned his smile. 'Okay.'

It was all he needed.

He caught her mouth with his. Their lips barely brushed and it was a seduction in gravity that had his pulse nosediving in an aeronautical spin. She tasted like a song in his mouth, sounded like music to his ears that was impossible to ignore. Tim held her as if she was his only home.

He dragged his lips from hers and stared at her. Cheeks rosy and flushed, her eyes sexily hooded, breathing in little pants, biting her lip. She looked like he felt—

completely lust-ridden—and more gorgeous than ever.

Then she flashed her wicked grin, and he grinned back. Their smiles pressed against each other as they settled in for a long, lingering kiss.

It soon turned into liquid heat with soft moans that trembled deep from her throat. He swallowed her flavour, her breath, all of her. He had never kissed anyone like this and dived deeper into heaven, silencing the eye of the storm.

***

She moaned when his lips touched hers, firm and hot. She couldn't stop and didn't want to stop. The longing to be with him had been deeply buried in a concrete bunker that had now been unlocked. Her hope chest's rusty lid had been flipped back, allowing her desire out. Free and thirsty.

The cocktails and Tim's flavour infused her senses. She gave into this madness, licking into his mouth, chasing his tongue. His earthy groan travelled through his chest and into hers. It made her pulse skip, reducing her inhalations into wild breathless pants.

Gasping, she dragged soupy air into her lungs, and opened her eyes.

Tim smiled at her.

He actually smiled a megawatt smile, with crinkles around his eyes that shone against his tanned skin. It was the true smile that belonged to the Tim she had always known and loved, with eyes the colour of the outback skies on sunrise—a light blue with fragments of green and gold in a complex kaleidoscope of colours.

It only made her thirstier.

She kissed him hard. Deep and long. The sweet sweeping strokes of his tongue had her drunk. Her heart hummed at the havoc he caused licking, touching, exploring her skin with the heat of his mouth and the coarseness of his workingman's hands. Rough. Gentle. Yet slow and smooth in movement.

She had to grip her fingers through his hair to stop herself from floating away under their mind-blowing chemistry, which sizzled through her bones. His teeth grazed over her pounding pulse, trekking his lips up her outstretched throat as it unzipped her icy soul, leaving her shields to melt in the summer sun.

How perfectly his mouth fitted against hers, claiming her. Owning her.

There were songs in his kisses she wanted to roll into a playlist that ran a lifetime on repeat.

He kissed her long and deep, making her lips numb, taking her from a slow simmer to an instant boil. And he was hard. Potent. And all male.

She climbed into his lap, leaving all of her sanity behind because this was a moment she'd dreamed of. A dream she'd never dared voice.

It was the best Christmas present she'd ever had. To be held in Tim's arms, have him loving her. Just her. All of her. And she would give him everything she had in return.

While the world howled outside, inside was their world. This was their time. It was only the two of them and tonight they only needed each other.

142

THIRTEEN

The weight of Monet's backpack made her hunch over, forcing her boots to sink further into the red mud as she approached her plane before dawn. 'Hello, Gertrude,' she said with relief, flashing her torch over the Cessna.

'Are you the star of your own show, surrounded by all of your groupies?' She smiled at the wallabies nestled under its wide wings.

'Thank you for keeping Gertrude safe,' she said to the heavens crowded with brilliant shining stars. There was no rain, no clouds. The cyclone had passed hours ago and she'd slept through it all, in the arms of Tim, who'd carried her to bed.

'Damn.' Monet fumbled in her step as the heated rush

washed over her at the memories of last night.

She'd always adored him fiercely—but always from afar. Now he would become her heart's undoing. The cause of an emotional slide she'd never recover from, because she'd broken her rule of sleeping with a friend.

What they'd done had ruined their friendship.

She wasn't going to put Tim in the position of trying to make small talk excuses as to why they could never be together. Monet was well aware of her faults. Faults Tim's mother used to say with one look every time Monet showed up.

Trying to forget and focus on what stood ahead of her, Monet stripped down the tarps and made quick work of unclipping the cables that secured her plane. Methodically, she went through her pre-flight checks.

That was the deal.

Contract completed.

This way she'd avoid any awkwardness from having slept with one of her friends. Sure, she'd always wanted to. But for Tim, Monet would only be a friend, because he had chosen Sherice for a wife.

What happened with Tim last night was because she was the only one there. They'd been drinking. And what else would you rather be doing in the middle of a cyclone?

But it had been good.

Damned best time of her life.

All of it was brilliant. From making crappy decorations, cooking dinner, to dancing around their silly tree, taking happy snaps. Then the finale of making love in the bathtub. Barely making it to her bedroom because there was no way she was sleeping in that messy bedroom of his.

Besides, the man was a broken-hearted mess, and this was just a freaking rebound for Tim. Nothing more.

She flicked on the radio to the sounds of Mickey's desperate voice squawking at her.

'Come in Double W One. This is Elsie Creek Tower. You there, Monet?' Mickey spoke with that much gravel in his voice as if he'd had a big night on the whiskey. But what made it worse was Mickey never used her name.

'Double W One here. Go ahead Elsie Creek Tower.'

'It's about bloody time. I was having a heart attack worrying about you, kid.'

Monet grinned as she finalised her pre-flight checks. Ready and raring to race away.

'Don't you laugh.'

'Good morning then.'

'There's nothing good about it.'

'Why, what's wrong?'

'First, are you and Gertrude okay?'

'Fine. Why?'

'Elsie Creek, the town, she got hit by the cyclone. And, um, kid, I'm sorry to tell you this, but the tree at the Inn...'

Oh no. She sat back hard. 'How bad is it?'

'We're waiting for daylight to assess it.'

She peered down the dark runway where dawn was

barely cracking on the distant horizon.

'Please tell me no one was inside?' She tossed her microphone onto the seat, pulled the cabin door shut and slammed the lever down on the safety lock.

Back in her seat, she flicked dials and switches, activating the spotlights that highlighted the airstrip. A few trees had fallen by the sides—but there was a herd of cattle blocking her plane's path.

Hmm, this wasn't her first rodeo on a runway.

She flicked at her dice and Chinese good luck travel charm as she nestled into her lamb's-wool seat cover, strapped on her belt, then punched the starter.

Gertrude's engine turned over beautifully. The propeller spun until it was invisible and that's when the little red plane purred.

She snapped on her navigation lights, the port and starboard lights cast an eerie glow over the wilderness. It made the lingering cattle take notice and do their thing where one moved, the next followed and so on. At this rate, in an hour she'd have the airstrip cleared, if she was lucky.

'The Inn was empty, kid,' said Mickey over the radio, 'Have you got Gertrude started?'

'I have. I'm on my way.'

'Hold on, kid, Marcus wants a chat. I'll patch him through. You there, Elsie Creek Police, over?'

'Elsie Creek Police to Double W One. Morning, Monet,' said Marcus's deep baritone over the headphones.

'Morning, Sarge, how can I help?'

'Can you check the roads on the way back to town?'

'I can.' She'd skim the dirt roads if she had to.

'Good. Elsie Creek's broken her banks and we've got more flash flooding coming. Look, I'm sorry about the Inn.'

'If you need me anywhere else, Marcus, just say it. I'll be wheels up in five.'

'Thank you. Because you're the only pilot I've got.'

'Where is everyone?'

'Check your calendar, they're all away for Christmas.'

Duh! She'd completely forgotten it was Christmas Day. *Merry bloody Christmas.*

'You tell me what you want, and Mickey and I'll work out a flight plan.' She flicked on her outdoor speakers. A blast of AC/DC did its best to spook the cattle. She flashed her spotlights on and off, steering down the sludgy runway searching for debris that would hinder her take-off. 'I've got a belly full of fuel and extra tanks on board, plus there's over a dozen stations I can raid for fuel if I need to do a station-hopping milk run. Just tell me where to go.'

Monet turned the plane at the base of the airstrip. It was a clear run ahead—as long as the wallabies didn't stray for the next five minutes.

She adjusted the plane's flaps, trying to predict the breeze, and checked her gauges as the final step of her take-off procedures.

'Good to know,' said Marcus. 'My officers are ringing everyone now, to see who needs help back to town and that everyone is safe. We've got no power and the creek's flooded the bridges and rail lines. Jax has got his fire crews setting up roadblocks, and the only thing big enough to move is—'

'Trucks.'

'Yeah. I've got Alex and Verily getting their road trains to clear the roads at first light. The Station Hand and his town crew are backing them up as a chainsaw gang in their utes. With you doing an aerial road report for me, I can organise the ground crew to help clear roads. I'd also appreciate regular checks on the main creek crossings around town. I don't want anyone getting caught in these flash floods. And I want you reporting in with Mickey every twenty.'

Normally she'd give the cop a whole load of cheek for giving her such a long shopping list, but not today. 'Done.'

'Every twenty minutes, Monet. No deviation for sight-seeing tours.'

Aww, he knew her so well. 'I'll let you know if I do, and only for a good cause.'

'Thank you,' Marcus said with a sigh of relief. 'Elsie Creek Police over and out.'

Highlighted by the dashboard's lights, Monet caught her reflection in the side window.

She was no longer that helpless little girl waiting for people to come to her aid. This time the tables had turned.

She punched the volume loud on her tablet. She

didn't like bells, but she played AC/DC's *Hells Bells* as loud as her speakers would go, with Angus Young's guitar solo jumpstarting her adrenalin.

'Let's party, Gertrude.' She cranked back on the controls, holding the plane in place, even though the runway was a slippery, muddy, ice rink. She needed to get in the air quick but keep the nose steady—which was a delicate balancing act—so she didn't flip the plane.

Monet watched the dials as the engine roared with vibration. At the last possible moment, she let the brakes go, catapulting her forward for a quick lift into the air.

It wasn't a textbook take-off. There were no textbooks for bush pilots, because every outback airstrip came with its own unique set of challenges, and today she was going to tap into every bit of that experience.

She wasn't going to let anyone else lose out on their Christmas, not if she could help it.

FOURTEEN

Tim heard the mechanical buzzing sound and then the music. He knew what it was without even opening his eyes. It was Monet leaving in her little red plane.

'Bugger.'

He rolled over in bed and face dived into the pillows where her fragrance lingered.

What had he done?

He'd slept with Monet.

Sure, over the years he'd been tempted, but never had they ever… until now. And right now, he wanted her again. Here, with him, where they wouldn't leave the house or this bed for the rest of the week.

But she was gone.

It was standard Monet operating procedure—to walk away.

If he'd been awake, would he have been able to convince her to stay? Would he have wanted her to?

He stumbled into the bathroom, flipping back the toilet seat. Cushions remained in his bathtub, that had been the best bath he'd ever had in his life, with or without water. Doused, scented candles filled the room with a warming floral aroma. They rested on the boxes that made up his cyclone kit, with their empty cocktail glasses sitting on the floor.

Daylight crept through the window. Birds sang in the dawn's pale pink and grey haze.

How bad was the damage?

Flushing the toilet, he washed his hands and scrubbed his face in the sink and paused to stare at the mirror. Written in the marker she'd used to draw on his windows was:

Enjoy the peace.
M.

No Xs for kisses. No Os for hugs. Nothing.

She'd given him exactly what he'd asked for—to be left alone so he'd have some peace and quiet.

Is that what he really wanted, to be left alone?

Showered, dressed and in the kitchen, he flicked on the kettle. As part of his daily routine, he peered through the window over the sinks.

A long-legged, black-necked stork, the Jabiru, elegantly waded through large puddles that had pooled in wide areas over the saturated lawn.

A shadow stretched from a mighty sea eagle, gliding above his shed where kites circled lazily on the breeze. In the distance horses grazed with scattered groups of cattle. All his sheds and outbuildings stood tall. Rigby Downs' homestead—at least—looked like it had survived the cyclone unscathed. But a closer inspection of the vast property would be needed to determine what he'd lost.

Relieved the rest seemed fine, Tim held his breath and searched through his kitchen window for that tawny frogmouth nest.

It was still there!

It must be a tough nest wedged in the groove of the tree that sheltered it from the storm. Both parents, with their grey-and-black-mottled feathers, blended perfectly with the bark of the tree, except for their yellow eyes and that death look as they watched the world below. The air buzzed with insects, taunting the fluffy chicks in the nest that snapped at the air. They'd survived.

Smiling to himself, a light-hearted sensation of hope filled his chest, bringing with it a sense of calm. It was the best he'd felt in ages.

Facing the kitchen, the table was clear from all the tools they'd used last night, leaving a singular wrapped present and an envelope.

A flash of light caught his eye in the lounge room, where the tin stars on his treetop flickered in the sunrise through the wall of windows. He grinned.

He liked that tree.

It looked even better in the daylight.

Making his soupy coffee, he sat at the table and opened his Christmas present wrapped in a simple brown paper bag.

He recognised Monet's writing on the envelope.

It reminded him of her weekly letters when he was doing his senior years at boarding school in Queensland. She'd tell him the town's gossip and he'd send her back postcards to make her laugh. Every year, she'd send him a Valentine's Day card too. He'd also send her little paint by numbers kits because she couldn't paint, addressed to *Claude Monet of the Unofficial Elsie Creek Inn.*

'Huh.' He glanced over to his shed's roof that was the canvas for her grown-up version of paint by numbers. Monet had certainly advanced from those days as a kid.

Again, he was reminded of the times he'd been confined to school campus on Sunday afternoons, and that's when he called Monet. It became a habit that lasted long after he'd graduated. Back then, he'd tell her all the things he'd been learning in his field of agri-science, the footy he played, the sights in the city.

While Monet stayed in Elsie Creek, getting her pilot's licence.

His dad used to say Monet had double the hours

required to work in a commercial airline, if she wanted it. But Monet hated the uniforms, the rules, and corporate pen-pushing policies that she said ruined all the fun in flying.

Monet didn't see it as a job, she just loved to fly; it was her freedom and her way to escape from anyone and everyone before she got trapped. Because she swore to never get trapped like she'd been on that Christmas Day, twenty years ago.

The silence was so much heavier now she'd left him.

The screen door creaked and there was Bandit poking his nose inside.

'Come on in.' He couldn't change the rules back, not now she'd left her mark on the place.

He patted his dog, sipped his coffee, then opened the present. 'What the—?' It was a princess barbie doll and his own mobile phone.

Why did Monet gift-wrap his phone?

He tore open the envelope and pulled out a card with a tiny red plane on the front cover. Inside, her neat handwriting said:

Hey there, Tim!
Merry-whatever-Day you want to make it.
I hope the Posh Prince likes his princess. You
can throw things at it for therapy. Kick it, or play
tug of war with Bandit.
Sorry, I couldn't find one with shiny cowboy
boots for you to cuddle in your sleep.

'Stuff that.' Tim threw it out the door where Bandit sniffed at it.

He then picked up the card to read the rest.

I know, it's a catty move on my part, but I just couldn't resist it. I was hoping you would have thrown it out the door by now.

'How did she know?' He looked around to see if she was spying on him.

The woman knew him as well as he knew her. How they'd never gotten together sooner was a mystery.

That's right, Monet didn't do relationships. Full stop.

She also didn't sleep with her friends. So, what did that make them today—especially since she'd flown away?

Opening the card again, he read:

Your actual gift is in your phone. I've downloaded an app for you that has a special playlist. You've got a year's subscription on me. Enjoy, and play it loud, young man. Play. It. Loud. Monet. xoxo

There were his Xs and Os.

He turned on his mobile phone to discover she'd changed his screensaver. Gone were the images of him and the ex, replaced with a scene of his shed's newly painted roof. In the background, his farm was highlighted by an amazing sunset.

He sat back, holding the phone out with a straight arm, inspecting the image.

He'd built that shed to give him something to focus on besides his hatred and disappointment in his cheating ex-fiancée.

Monet had obviously realised why he'd done it. That's why she'd painted his shed, to remind him of what he loved most—this station.

To Tim, it wasn't a job but a lifestyle he truly loved.

Monet would have known this from all those hours he'd spent talking with her about his plans. Years of planning, where he'd come to depend on her brutally truthful responses, especially with figures. Not only as his bookkeeper, but as someone with a bountiful knowledge of other stations in the area, seen from her bird's-eye view. He'd always respected her opinion.

God, he missed her.

The year he'd cut her off hurt. On Sundays, he was forever catching himself reaching for the phone to call her, or send her a random email.

It hurt she'd left him now.

Following Monet's instructions from the card, Tim activated the new phone app, which directed him to the one and only playlist she'd named:

The Posh Prince's Playlist.

He opened it up and grinned, his eyes widening as he scrolled down the list of artist's names, bands, and songs that kept going and going.

'No way.'

It had to be every single song he'd ever had Monet smuggle in for him. It was a playlist trip down memory lane. It was all of the music he'd blast when he was down the track, well away from his mum, doing the boundary fence and bore runs.

Trips to town were another sacred time when he'd belt out the music while singing at the top of his lungs, as if in his own rock concert.

He used to play music all the time while still a station hand, working under his father's watchful eye.

Back then he was just part of the crew. He always knew he'd be the owner one day, with his father preparing for retirement. They'd invested in his mum's unit near the beach so his dad could fish while she shopped.

His father was supposed to be there when Tim called for weekly beer sessions, seeking his wise words of wisdom. But that heart attack had stripped away all of their plans and that's when Tim had turned off the music and cut off his best friend.

He missed her more as the minutes dragged by.

Pressing shuffle on the music, he scrolled over to her Instagram handle, searching for last night's selfies. He soon found their wide smiles that shone in their eyes. It had been an amazing night, created from nothing that led to something more.

Could they call what they'd done a moment of weakness?

No. Not when it had been such an intense moment between them. He'd read it in her eyes, the same way she could always read him.

Unless she'd let him be with her purely as a rebound thing, to grow or heal or something? Whatever happened, he felt better for it. Is that why she walked away?

Monet had left him over a year ago without fighting for their friendship and here she was, again, flying away.

Sure, he wanted to be left alone, but why did this feel ten times worse than anything his ex had ever done to him? Why did it feel like someone had wrenched his heart out to follow the smoke trails of that little red plane?

Why did it feel like he'd lost his soul?

Damn her for making him feel again.

Damn her for doing what he asked.

Damn her for leaving him.

The house phone rang and he knew who it was—not who he wanted it to be. Remaining seated, he snagged the phone from its cradle on the wall. 'Merry Christmas, Mum.'

'Darling, are you okay?'

'Fine. Just opening my present.'

'Who? What?'

He smiled at his gift on his mobile and realised, for

the first time in his life, that Monet herself was a gift.

'What did that crazy girl do now?'

He frowned. 'Mum, Monet isn't crazy.'

'Of course she is, and so is her mother. She got to you, didn't she? I knew it.'

'She's not even here. Monet's gone.' He rubbed his chest, now heavy with an emptiness that echoed at the words. Monet had left him.

'Good riddance.'

He frowned, inhaling deeply through his nose. 'If you want me to hang up, Mum, I will.'

'What has gotten into you?'

'Don't you dare ever say another nasty thing about Monet again. Do you hear me? Oh, and we had a great time last night, for Christmas Eve.' They'd created a new tradition that was everything anti-Mum. Did he dare tell his mother that and ruin her Christmas?

'I see.'

'What I don't get is why you hate her so much? Dad was always good to Monet. Why weren't you?'

'I wasn't mean to her.'

'Bull. Tell me now or I'll hang up and won't speak to you until you tell me why. Today.' He slapped his forehead. He sounded just like his mother!

It was a good thing Monet wasn't there, or she'd give him curry over it.

'I'm waiting.' He sipped his coffee and reached back into the fridge, finding another box of tofu sitting on top of his plate of barbecued steak. Monet never told him what she'd cooked with it and he didn't want to know. Flicking it off the plate, he grabbed a chunk of flame grilled steak. 'I haven't got all day, Mum. I need to do a property assessment on the damage.' Did he dare radio Monet to come back and do a flyover?

'It was Emma.'

'The cyclone?'

'No, Emma. Monet's mother.'

'I don't remember her.'

'Do you remember Tucker?'

'Yeah, he lived here for a bit. Tucker taught me how to ride my motorbike.'

'Until he married Emma and they got their own station.'

The station that no one lived on, with the house bulldozed to the ground. Very few people realised Monet still owned all that land. She'd been leasing it to Tim and his dad to run their cattle on that station for decades, at a ridiculously cheap mate's rate.

Monet told no one. Especially his mother.

'What has that got to do with you picking on Monet?'

'I didn't—'

'You did. You were always rude to her. Why, Mum? You have five minutes.' By then he'd have eaten his plate of meat, fed the dog, finished his cuppa and would be ready to face the day. Later than normal, but he felt good.

Really good.

'It was Tucker.' Her tone softened as she said, 'I-I cared about him—'

'Oh, no, you didn't.' He winced, shifting in his seat. He now understood what Monet had been hinting at. 'You were jealous of Emma because you loved Tucker. Didn't you?' First his ex, now his mother? This was going to scar him for life.

The other end of the phone was silent.

'Did Dad know?'

'No. And I never cheated on your father, just... Tucker had this way about him.'

'I don't want to know.' Tim screwed his face up in horror, tossing his half-eaten piece of steak to the dog and putting the rest back into the fridge. Appetite destroyed.

'I couldn't help it.'

'Yes, you could.' He sneered at the phone, slapping the fridge shut. 'That's a weak excuse and you know it. Instead, you took it out on Monet for most of her life, especially when she needed someone. A little girl who grew up always making sure she was there for me, but *you* made me push her away.'

Again, his mother remained silent.

'*You* told me I couldn't see her anymore. Were you jealous Monet was Emma and Tucker's daughter, and not yours?' His parents had him late in life having had lots of trouble conceiving.

'I didn't want you marrying her, or being with her. Monet's family's genes are all wrong. Her mother is crazy—

,

'Monet's mother is living an amazing life in Spain.'

'Rubbish! They committed that woman to the nuthouse.'

'I will only tell you this once,' he said in a low tone. 'Monet's mother voluntarily went to get help. When that flood trapped them in that house, Emma was suffering with postnatal depression that was magnified by her bipolar. Her husband had disappeared, drowned, and her newborn son had died from complications due to being born prematurely. Have some sympathy for the poor woman.'

'Tucker was too good for her,' snapped his mother, who never knew when to stop. 'You mark my words, that Monet will end up just like her mother.'

'See, that's where you're wrong. Monet may be a little eccentric in some ways, but she's not nuts,' said Tim. 'She is perfectly normal.' His Monet was imperfectly perfect.

'How would you know?'

'I was with her when she had tests at the clinic in Brisbane, when I was at boarding school.' He'd sat beside her in the specialist's office, holding Monet's trembling hand, seeing her true fear of the future. That day, he'd sworn to her they'd never change as friends, no matter what the test results said.

'Billions of people suffer from bipolar disorder. It's more common than you think, and with the right treatment, they live perfectly normal lives,' Tim told his mother. 'You're still stuck with that old stigma that mental health is somehow their fault and that inflicting punishment upon them will cure it. Well, you're wrong. They're just people who deal with issues in a different way. They're still people.'

'You didn't tell me you'd been with Monet to do some medical tests. What else did she make you do with her? I know she helped you keep secrets from me.'

It was Monet who looked after his music, and there was no way he'd tell her he'd slept with Monet.

But now, for the first time, he stood up for Monet against his mother.

Yet, Monet had done it all her life. Standing tall, facing down all those stares and whispers, when there was nothing wrong with her. His dad used to say she was *Teflon tough*.

But Tim had seen those moments when Monet's shields were down, when her vulnerability showed itself, raw and wounded. She never showed anyone but him that side of her.

That's when he'd haul her up to the roof of the Inn to stare at the stars, to talk or not say anything. He'd tried his hardest to do something with her so she'd forget her troubles. Just like she did for him.

And how did he repay her?

With a year of silence.

Well, not anymore. Now fighting the urge to get into his ute and chase after her. But where would she be?

'Look, darling, you deserve better than that, you have Sherice—'

'Who cheated on me with my best mate!' He then realised—wasn't Monet meant to be with his mate, Marcus too? *Oh, no!*

'She slipped. It happens.'

'Yeah, like you wanted to do with Tucker over my

father.' Tim sneered with the rupturing bubble of hate and hurt rising like a fire in his chest. 'Now I understand why you were so forgiving towards Sherice.' He stood up from the table, his chair scraping across the floor to slam against the cupboard. 'Merry Christmas, Mum, but this conversation is over.' He hung up the phone and pulled the plug on the damned thing.

Booting the door open, he snatched up his hat and headed outside. Emotions sucked, and getting involved with people who toyed with your emotions was worse. He was done with women. 'Ho freaking ho!'

FIFTEEN

Inside his new shed, music carried from the speakers in Tim's ute as he re-sharpened his chainsaw. Having returned from a basic check on the property, he was glad he'd gotten away with minimal damage from the cyclone with only a few fallen trees and some damaged fencing.

The music kept him company as each new track came on and he smiled at the memories certain songs brought up. Again, he fought the strong urge to get in his ute and chase after Monet—only to stop short and scowl at her for being with Marcus.

Monet wasn't a cheater. And neither was he.

But was she?

It was wrong. Just wrong.

A loud horn blared in his yard, and a set of shiny steel smoke stacks rose from the crest on the track belonging to a road train. It was Alex.

Tim waved as he strolled out to greet his mate, turning the massive truck around. 'You're running a bit light there, mate?' He pointed to the lack of trailers that normally snaked behind the semi-engine.

'Why don't you answer your bloody phone,' said Alex, jumping down from the truck's cab.

'I've been out. Merry Christmas.'

'Yeah, you too.' They shook hands and man-hugged like old mates.

'Want a beer?'

'Nah, I'm driving. A coffee would be good.'

'I've got plenty of that up at the house and all this other tucker Monet baked. Careful, though, she's snuck some tofu in there somewhere.' He never did pay Monet for all her food. He was such a selfish prick.

'Is Monet still experimenting with her food?' Alex asked, as they wiped their boots on the mat by the kitchen door.

'Yeah, and are you still cooking for Verily?' Tim flicked the kettle on as they both scrubbed their hands in the sink.

Alex let rip a wide grin. 'I like cooking for Verily. We share the chores in our house.'

Tim never had to do household chores with his mother around. Yet, these past few days, Monet had made sure he'd done his fair share of chores, even though he was technically the boss.

'Hey, I like your tree.' Alex nodded to the lounge.

'Me too,' he replied, grinning at the ugly thing. 'We made it last night. It was home delivered, caught it right out the back door.'

'Efficient.'

'Here, coffee thick enough to make the spoon stand.'

'Ta. Need it. We've been clearing roads all morning. Didn't you hear?' Alex reached out and flicked at the phone's unplugged cable. 'Dare I ask?'

'Exes and mothers.'

Alex nodded.

'What did I miss?' Tim asked.

'Elsie Creek broke her banks, and the town got hit hard. We lost power around midnight. Back home we've lost a few mango trees in the orchard, but...' Alex dropped his Akubra onto the spare chair, slumped into his seat at the table, slurping on his coffee. 'Have you spoken to Monet, yet?'

'Not since she flew out at dawn. Why? Where is she?' His heart pounded with fear for her. 'Is she okay?' Did she fly straight back to Marcus?

'The Inn got hit.'

'How?'

'That tree.'

'Oh no.' Tim flopped hard onto his chair. 'Was anyone in there? Monet would be devastated if anyone got hurt.'

'No one was in there. I don't think Monet's seen it yet, she's been too busy running regular road reports for Marcus.'

'They make quite the team, Marcus and Monet.' Didn't that bring his emotions to a screaming halt.

'Yeah, who would've thought it? Monet, assisting the cop.' Alex gave a quick laugh and said, 'She's been bloody brilliant.'

'How?'

'The flash flooding has cut off lots of people, and with more water on the way that little plane of hers has been hauling people and supplies all morning.'

While Tim had been loping around the farm having a private singalong. Thank goodness he'd asked her to stay last night. 'Do you need a hand?'

'I was hoping you'd say that.' Alex grinned, holding up his mug. 'Can we have that with coffee and tucker to go?'

'I'll even chuck in a few beers for the occasion, seeing the pub is shut.'

'Not today, it isn't. The publican opened her pub's doors at daylight. Samantha's got women and children staying there with all her staff on deck. Lucy's hauled her coffee van into town and people are meeting back on Main Street. It's a freaking post-cyclone street party and you're invited.'

'I'm in. Do you need some chains?'

'A chainsaw with fuel will do.'

Tim did a sweep of the house, locked it up, fed the dog and loaded up the truck.

'I like your roof.' Alex pointed to the large painted Brahman wearing a blue ribbon. 'Did you hire the town's secret roof tagger, or get someone in to do it?'

'Erm… It was my gift to me.'

'Huh?'

'It's the money I would've spent on that engagement ring you stopped me from buying that day on the highway.'

Alex removed his Akubra and scrubbed at his hair. 'Worst conversation of my life.'

'Mine too.' When Alex had told Tim his future-wife was cheating on him, Tim had wanted to kill him.

What followed was a blur to finish the muster, then a hazy vacuum of nothingness until the pocket rocket landed on his doorstep. Damn, he missed her.

But he shouldn't, not while Monet was with Marcus. He didn't want to think about it—he'd hate her and himself as the guilt already clawed at his guts for what they'd done

Climbing into Alex's truck, they hit the road for town.

Along the way, they cut down thick branches that were hazardous to vehicles. Using chains, they dragged trees that had fallen across the dirt roads, their jeans covered in gravelly red mud as the two men cleared roads in their region.

Back in the truck, cruising down the wide dirt road, they both ducked as the red plane, with its straw broom painted along the underbelly, swooped low above them.

Tim smiled wide as the heat in his chest grew at the familiar sight.

Alex snatched up his radio's handpiece while steering the beast on wheels. 'Is that the *Wicked Witch of the Westerly Winds* who just buzzed me.'

'Hey there, Alex,' Monet's husky voice carried over the radio's speakers and filled the cab. 'You look naked without any trailers kicking up dust behind you. Where are you headed?'

'Back to town. Why?'

'Leviathan Creek's coming up fast and I've got supermum, Karen Kimble and her tribe about ten clicks ahead of you. I would collect them, but I'm needed at the Barnes's, they've got an injured kid.'

'No worries. Does Karen have all of her kids with her?'

'Looks like it. Her van's stuck in front of Leviathan Creek. She can't cross it, and she can't go back home because all of the other creeks in her area have flooded behind her. It's the same story everywhere, and the floodwaters haven't peaked yet. So, take this as your personalised flying traffic report in the sky... this will be your last run, Alex. Those creeks have become rivers that are rising fast. If you're not careful, you won't get back into town either.'

Tim and Alex frowned at each other, shaking their heads.

'Like hell,' said Alex over the radio. 'We're heading back now.'

'Outstanding, young man. I'll tell the Station Hand and his groupies. They're trying to rig up something to get to Karen and the kids if I couldn't land. So perfect timing, my friend.'

'Thanks.'

'Hey, did you check up on Tim for me?'

Tim smiled widely at Alex. She cared.

'Yep, I even dragged him back into the cab with me.'

'Good. About time you stepped off that station, cowboy. Don't play too hard, boys. Over and out.'

Tim needed to talk to her. With his eyes on the sky, he watched the little red plane bank to the left. Monet sounded normal and busy.

The closer they got into range, the more radio chatter flooded the airways until Monet's voice sliced through, alerting them that Alex's semi was on its way.

Alex grinned at Tim and said, 'I kind of feel like a hero coming to their rescue, huh?'

'In slow motion in this hunk of metal.'

Alex patted the truck's dashboard like a pet. 'Hush your mouth, she's tough enough to take on a crocodile-infested river.'

'You watch too much YouTube.' Tim chuckled, then pointed ahead where half a dozen kids waved at them in the middle of the road. 'There's the Kimble's van.'

Alex tooted his loud horn, sending birds from the

nearby scrublands flocking to the skies. If they'd done that any sooner, it would've been a hazard for Monet in her plane. The kids continued to scare the wildlife as they jumped up and down vigorously.

'You guys are my freaking heroes,' cried out Karen, grabbing her baby from the capsule as she climbed out of the van.

Alex parked his massive semi nearby and Tim jumped down. 'What are you doing out here, Karen?'

'We were trying to get back to their father. I just didn't expect the river to come up so fast. Monet was planning to land on the road when she spotted the truck.'

'Where is your husband?' Alex asked, as he joined them, leaving the truck's engine running.

'*Work*. Seriously. At work! Forget the family, or that's its Christmas Day. Nooo, my husband had to go and check on the bloody mine site, didn't he! Got the call at four a.m. from that fancy schmancy mine manager in Sydney—'

'Okay, Karen,' said Tim, with palms up as if approaching a wild animal. 'Let's get you and the kids into the truck.'

'Thank you.' She dragged on Tim's shirt, bringing him down and engulfing him in a strong hug that smelt of baby powder and the giggles of a baby girl. She did the same to Alex. 'I'm gonna hug that Monet so freaking hard when I see her too. That girl has been saving people left, right and centre.'

'Really?' Tim asked, helping the seven boys of

differing ages to scramble into Alex's truck.

'You should hear that Mickey going off at her.'

'Nothing new there, Mickey's always a cranky old coot,' said Tim.

'This is worse,' said Karen. 'Mickey's been telling Monet off for using dirt roads and driveways as airstrips. He reckons it'll strip her undercarriage and wreck the tyres. It's been fascinating to listen to. We've got Marcus getting regular road reports from her, like how they do those traffic jams in the city. They make a great team, Monet and Marcus,' Karen said, climbing into the truck.

'Yeah, right?' Tim wiped away the scowl. He shouldn't be jealous of Marcus being with Monet. He liked Marcus, and he wanted Monet to be happy. But the jealousy burned his chest and made his stomach harden. Did he dare tell Marcus what he'd done with Monet?

He needed to talk to Monet soon. Hopefully, before he saw Marcus.

'Kids! Shoes off and no dirty feet on the bunk,' hollered Karen, climbing up the passenger side of the large truck. 'We're guests. Make room for your baby sister while I get in my seat.'

'I've never had this many kids in my truck before,' said Alex, getting in behind the wheel.

'This is your future softball team there, mate,' said Tim, climbing into the passenger seat and shutting them all inside.

Seven boys wrestled each other to find the best spot

to lie on their stomachs in the bunk bed. They eagerly watched Alex steering the massive truck as it started rolling down the dirt road leaving Karen's van behind.

'Is it true that the Unofficial Elsie Creek Inn got destroyed?' Karen asked from her seat in the middle, holding the baby girl.

'All I saw was that the Inn's tree is down over the house and right across the road, you can't get around it,' replied Alex. 'Marcus and his officers were taping the area off, diverting traffic. They couldn't spare the manpower to cut it up and clear the road—not with all the flooding.'

'I heard. Elsie Creek's broken her banks,' said Karen. 'The last floods we had people died.'

No one said a word. But Tim knew they were thinking of Monet.

They drove through the first flooded crossing, where the water ran halfway up the semi's massive tyres.

'Leviathan Creek is running fast,' Tim said from his heightened position in the cab. It was a rushing white-water rafting river. He'd love to kayak it, if he were game enough to float alongside the crocodiles spread along the far banks.

'It's got a strong current too,' said Alex with a tight grip on the steering wheel. 'Monet was right, if we'd left it any later, we wouldn't be able to get through.'

'Wasn't Monet farm-sitting your place over Christmas, like normal?' Karen asked Tim.

'She was.'

'Why didn't you go to Perth? Hey, where have you

been? Have you been avoiding us because of that Shiny Sherice?'

'Shiny Sherice? Where did that come from?' Tim asked Karen.

'Verily. She's our pitching and fielding softball coach, isn't she Alex?' said Karen, nudging Alex in the ribs. Then she turned her attention back to Tim. 'But you'd know that if you didn't snob-off on us.'

'I was busy with the muster and stuff.'

'Tim's got a new shed, and he even got a sign writer for the roof too,' said Alex. 'It looks good, suits the place.'

'Talking about roofs, did you hear,' Karen said, 'the cop shop got tagged. Marcus was spewing.'

'Yeah, what was the picture?' Tim asked. What sort of relationship was Monet in with Marcus if she was keeping secrets from the cop, graffitiing his workplace?

'Long arm of the law. It looks good, and for once we could actually see it from the ground the way the cop shop's roof is slanted from the airport side. Everyone went to take a look. Which, of course, upset Mickey having all those people walking all over his precious flight path. The place has gone all arty since Kat came back. I mean, who didn't get one of Kat's candles for Christmas? We've got the tea house museum, the tinman, and now a roof tagger. Who do you think the roof artist is?' Karen asked all in one breath.

'No idea,' said Alex.

'Don't look at me, I haven't been into town in ages,' Tim added, although he was keen to see Monet's artwork.

'Stop that, okay?' She wagged her finger at Tim like the mother she was. 'People care about you. And we're friends. You just say the word and there's a bunch of us willing to bitch-slap Shiny Sherice for you.'

'Thanks, Karen.' He slid his arm around her and gave her a tender squeeze. 'It's nice to feel wanted.'

'You know, Monet would be the first to do the honours in happy-tapping your ex. Hey, you know you broke her heart, right?'

'Who did what to who?' Alex arched his eyebrow at Tim, both men a head and shoulders taller than Karen in the middle.

Tim wanted to jump out of the cab.

'Monet's always had a thing for Tim,' said Karen, cradling her baby. 'Way back in school, when she followed you around like a puppy.'

'She did not.'

'It's true, Monet did, mate,' said Alex.

'I thought she'd gotten over it when you went to boarding school, but I know,' said Karen, nodding.

'Know what?' Tim could just slap himself for asking.

'Monet was devastated when you started seeing Sherice,' said Karen. 'Then when you got engaged, Monet just up and left us without telling anyone. She just left her usual laminated message on the open door of the Inn, like normal. None of us had realised she'd actually skipped the country to go to Spain.'

'Monet went and visited her mother. That had

nothing to do with me.'

'She could have gone and seen her mother anytime. Monet just made sure she wasn't in town for your engagement party. Did you even invite her?'

No, he didn't. 'She wasn't here.'

'Convenient, huh?' Karen said, rather smugly with chin raised as they approached the next river crossing. 'Oh, jeez, are we gonna make it?' She grabbed Tim's hand and squeezed it tight. 'Boys, hug a brother.'

'There's Dad,' cried one of the youngsters, pointing to the far bank where a group of men and assorted utes had gathered. All of the vehicles wore thick red mud flicked along their sides.

'Sit back,' Tim ordered the excited young boys. They were distracting Alex, who needed to concentrate on his driving. 'Here, give me the baby.' He grabbed the baby girl from Karen who gripped his arm tightly.

'Why don't you have seatbelts in this truck?' complained Karen.

'I don't normally carry passengers,' replied Alex. 'Calm down, Karen. You're upsetting your kids.'

'Settle down boys, it's gonna be okay. Alex and I've been through bigger rivers than this, eh, Alex,' said Tim.

Alex nodded at Tim with wide eyes, both lying through their teeth. This was the type of river they'd watch from the banks, drinking beer while waiting for the water levels to drop. But they didn't have that luxury today.

Leviathan was a kiddie pool compared to the

mammoth of rushing water before them. The run-off from Elsie Creek was a river, rushing at a neck-breaking speed.

'Tim, where do I go, mate? You know this road better than me.' Alex didn't take his eyes off the river, forcing his way down through the gears to slow the truck right down.

'Aim for the right, there's a washout on the left. They fill it in every year, but with the way that water's ripping through, all that new topsoil will be long gone.' And they did not want to hit that hole. If they did it would cause the cab to tilt and risk having the current push them over.

A surge of protectiveness rushed over Tim as he held the cute baby girl to his chest. Meanwhile, Karen kept a death-grip on his arm.

'You'll miss it from here, now go straight, easy mate,' instructed Tim as Alex drove through. If they bogged it, they were stuffed. This river had some big crocodiles.

A log banged into the side of the cab and the boys squealed as loud as their mother.

'Your poor truck,' said Karen.

'She'll be right,' Alex said, with a white-knuckle grip on the steering wheel. 'This truck's been through worse.'

'H-h-how is your dad?' Karen asked, trying to deflect her fear. She reached back to touch her boys huddled together on the bunkbed like cheeky cockatoos on a power line.

'Dad's good. I spoke to him this morning. He's having a holiday in Bris-Vegas,' said Alex, slowly steering them through the raging river.

The sound of rushing water was deafening. The temperature dropped as water splashed up the side of the driver's door sending a fine mist through the cab.

The drive went on forever. Inching their way through the flood waters, they slowly climbed up the other side, where everyone breathed a sigh of relief.

The truck's brakes hissed as water poured from her sides, trickling down the muddy road and back to the crossing. Men rushed to greet them at the doors to help unload the boys, mother and baby.

'*Daddy*,' cried out all seven boys as they rushed to their father.

'Thank you, boys,' said Karen, with the baby in her arms, again hugging both Tim and Alex. She then turned to her husband with a scary scowl. 'YOU! How dare you leave your family on Christmas—' Her husband silenced her with a kiss and one enormous family group hug.

Alex and Tim leaned against the cab of the truck, watching Karen and her mob reunite with their dad. All of them vying to hug the guy, then hug each other, delighted to be together again.

It showed how beautiful love could be from a distance, and how messy it was up close. It was powerfully magic.

'Would you ever want something like that?' Tim asked Alex.

'Yeah, but not that many. I guess I'll have to get used to it soon enough,' he said, trying to wipe away his grin.

'What? You and Verily?'

Alex grinned wider.

'Since when?'

'It was my Christmas present.'

'Congratulations, mate.' Tim shook Alex's hand, heartily patting his friend on the back.

Alex was beaming with pride. 'Thanks. It wasn't planned, it just happened. Molly can't wait, she's already online shopping for baby gear, while Verily's cruisy as normal. She's in her truck doing the roads on the other side of town. I couldn't stop her if I tried. Hopefully, she will be back in town by now.' Alex checked his watch and headed back to the truck's cab. 'Oh, by the way, you're gonna be the godfather and honorary uncle,' he said, pointing at Tim. 'I'm booking it in now, so you'll always feel obligated to give me access to fish your billabongs.'

'Anytime mate, you don't need an invitation to visit or go fishing. I'm honoured.' *Huh, a godfather.*

Alex inhaled deep, his chest rising and falling as he shook his head. 'I've got to admit, it's scary and exciting all at the same time. Me, a father. I hope I'm better at it than my old man.'

'You two are getting on now, aren't you?'

'Oh yeah. Weekly calls and he'll stop over whenever he's in town.'

'How's the brewery going?' Tim asked, climbing back into the truck's cab.

'With the baby coming, I was going to put it on hold,'

said Alex, sliding in behind the wheel, 'but Verily wants to move everything forward.'

'How?'

'We were meant to have the official beer launch party at the pub on New Year's Eve. But with what happened last night, Verily and I agreed with Samantha to launch the Rosella beer this afternoon as part of the town's cyclone-Christmas street party. As of today, our Rosella beer is officially on the market.'

'That's brilliant, mate.'

'When you get a chance, you should come check out the vats we've got in the refurbished packing shed. You won't recognise the place.'

'I can't wait. What about the rest of your plans?'

'Verily's coaching clinics are booked out with a waiting list. And I'm waiting on the certifications for an organic brewery, which will be easier when I grow our own crops. I want to do the planting at the end of this wet and I'd love your learned opinion on that.'

'I said I'd help you. So, it's all finally happening, eh?' Tim patted his friend on the shoulder, who put the massive truck into gear. It rolled slowly behind the line of utes, all heading back to town. 'Congratulations. I mean that, mate. Congratulations.'

Tim glanced back in the large side mirror where the Kimble family reunion was still going on loud and messy, but heart-warming to see. One big family. It's what he wanted.

'I'd never planned it,' said Alex over the truck's engine noise. 'Kids, family. I mean, I was only thinking of my brewery. I didn't plan on meeting Verily and now being a dad. None of it. But I'm so glad it's happening, all of it.'

'Yeah…' Tim sat back in his seat and fought back the need to frown. He was happy for his mate.

Tim had always planned on having a family, but all his plans fell apart and he found himself home alone. He'd thought it's what he wanted, but seeing Karen and her family made him realise he didn't want to be alone anymore.

'Are we going back to town?' Tim wanted to see Monet. With the Inn being damaged, he wanted to be there for her when she landed.

She'd been there for him countless times, it was now Tim's turn to be there for her. Even if she didn't want it. Even if she was with Marcus. Tim had been Monet's friend first. If Monet wanted more, so be it. Tim wasn't scared of Marcus—he was more frightened of losing Monet.

SIXTEEN

The view from her pilot's seat was truly remarkable, where Monet glided over the town of Elsie Creek with its images painted on various expansive rooftops.

It was an eclectic show of 2D poster art in full display from the skies. She still got a kick out of it every time she saw them. Her, Monet, the kid who couldn't do stick figures and failed arts and crafts, did these spray-painted pictures.

There was the Mad Hatter, giving shade to a teacup and saucer on the tea house roof. A retro 50s glamorous women in curlers stretched over the hairdressing shop. A mail-laden snail raced over the post office roof. There was a cracked spanner in the works for the hardware store and the latest, the strong arm of the law for the police station.

The large painted images, covering selective small business roofs, stood boldly under the sunshine, reminding her of the street art spotted on the side of buildings in the city. Except in Elsie Creek, the only place big enough for that kind of art was the roof. Perfect for a pilot's bird's-eye view.

Monet stifled a grin as her passengers eagerly pointed out the window. She felt like a tour guide flying above a zoo.

Groups of people had gathered at the pub's intersection in the town's main street. The iconic building sat opposite the train station and the small town park. The surrounding roads and railway lines were all hidden under water, turning the town of Elsie Creek into an island and it looked like everyone was there, ready to celebrate.

'Oh, no. A tree fell over that house, Mummy,' cried out the little boy with his two front teeth missing.

'I'm so sorry, Monet,' said Anna, sitting in the seat beside her son.

'It's okay, it's not your fault.' Monet frowned at the enormous tree that had once stood tall and proud, now lying on its side covering her whole Inn, blocking off the road.

Monet didn't blame anyone. Trees had fallen down all over the place. There were corridors of trees tossed aside like toothpicks from the cyclone's destructive force.

No one got hurt. And that's what mattered the most.

She reached into the front hatch for her candy canes. 'Hey, you kids. Don't say I never give you anything,' she said, passing back her secret stash.

Anna looked at Monet questioningly.

'It's for the air pressure on their ears, it helps.' Monet single-handily unwrapped her own candy cane in one well-practised move.

The little plane was full of people with their overnight bags. Three kids wore excited grins, ripping open the candy wrappers. They were seated in the back with their sleeping dog, an inquisitive new puppy, a pair of worried parents, and poor little Robbie who had his arm in a sling. She didn't need a medical degree to see he'd broken it.

Monet flew over the hospital and spotted the ambulance waiting for her near the runway. It was the third time today.

An elderly couple had an asthma scare and Marcus wanted them back because of the floods. The rest were kids she'd brought back to town after they'd hurt themselves with their Christmas presents. Bikes seemed to be the major cause.

At least young Robbie had enough sense to wear his new bike helmet, but he'd been too quick on the fly, to listen to his dad.

Monet could relate. She remembered her first flying lesson, being in too much of a rush to get out there and do her thing.

Her thing today, so far, had been dozens of pickups and deliveries, station hopping from one airstrip to the next. She would collect one mob of people to hang with another group, ensuring no one was alone on Christmas Day. She brought in people and took out extra supplies, all courtesy of Marcus's instructions and his office of cops, all working overtime.

The new fire chief, Jax, and his team had also pitched in, with everyone getting involved. They all helped each other, checking on neighbours, families and friends to ensure everyone was okay. The town's community spirit was strong, and today's exceptional view was a beautiful thing to see.

Monet spotted Alex and Verily's trucks lined up on the edge of town, which meant Tim was in town. At least he wasn't home alone on the station. But she wasn't looking forward to seeing him again; it was going to be awkward.

And Monet didn't do awkward.

She'd rather walk away from that party, avoiding it and Tim altogether.

What was she worried about? Tim wouldn't bother with her anymore. Especially now her job at Rigby Downs was done, and she was still on the clock busily working for another company.

'Check your seatbelts, guys, and hold onto your toys tightly because we're going in for a landing.' Monet zoomed down to the tarred runway with its white line painted down the middle.

It was a cakewalk compared to the sloppy airstrips and cavity crackers she'd been landing on all day. Mud still stuck to the underbelly of the plane, she could feel it weighing them down.

But Gertrude never missed a beat.

Wheels down, they landed so smoothly it was as if they'd been driving on the tarmac all along.

'Are we there yet?' Hollered the girl with a cheek full of candy.

'We are. Welcome to Elsie Creek. And, on behalf of Gertrude and myself, we'd like to thank you for flying Double W airways, the broom in the sky.'

The kids showed off their goofy grins with candy canes hanging out of their mouths as Monet taxied closer to the hangar where the ambulance waited for them.

Gertrude's engine wound down with the jolt of silence.

Monet sucked on her candy cane like a cigar as she opened the centre door, dropped the stairs and like a well-trained hostess, helped her passengers disembark.

Anna hugged her. 'Thank you, Monet. We'll never forget this.'

'You guys be safe.' She waved to the family climbing into the ambulance.

Mickey approached her, wiping his sweaty brow with the towel the same colour as his grey overalls. He wheezed as he dragged his trolley filled with fuel drums and tools.

'Where's your nifty buggy?' She asked, helping him to drag it closer to Gertrude.

'The coppa pinched it.'

'A cop stole it?'

'He's got some schmancy word for it, but I'm telling you now, kid, take a break,' he said in his gravelly tone that always sounded annoyed.

'Why? I'll give you a hand to refuel.'

'I said, you and Gertrude are on a break.''

She looked at her watch. 'There's still plenty of daylight.'

Mickey's nifty golf buggy, that they used to taxi planes and fuel, rolled up with Marcus, in his police uniform.

'Did you steal Mickey's toy?' Monet asked the cop. 'I hope your department is paying him? You've got this poor old man dragging all the avgas by hand.'

'I'm not old, or bloody helpless, kid.'

'There are too many people on the street for me to drive my car in there,' said Marcus. 'Don't worry, Mickey's getting cash and grog for lending me his toy.'

'Marcus, the kid needs a break,' said Mickey, removing fuel lines from his trolley. 'We'll be breaking flight laws if she doesn't have a break.'

'Come on, Monet. I've been stretching the grey lines of the law all bloody day, this one I won't.' Marcus patted the buggy's vacant passenger seat. 'I'm doing a coffee run. Does my favourite bush pilot want one?'

'The only pilot available, you mean—heck, yeah. Mickey, want me to shout you a cuppa?'

'And one of the Caveman's steak sangas he's got goin' on. I can smell 'em from here.'

'My treat for commandeering your golf buggy,' said Marcus.

'Told yah he had a fancy word for it. Now, nick off so I can refuel and wash this muck off this poor plane's underbelly.' Mickey leaned over to peer beneath the plane where it was covered in dry mud. 'You're bloomin' crazy, kid, for landin' on half of them dirt roads. I reckon you're carrying enough mud on here to build yourself a dozen ant mound radio towers.'

'I'll get you two of everything then, that should keep you happy,' she said to the grouchy man. 'Is everyone accounted for?' Monet asked Marcus as he drove them toward the heart of town.

'We're waiting on a few to return from the mine.'

They drove down the main street, the town's shop windows were still filled with garish Christmas displays, but their view was marred by the now familiar X stretched over their glass panels. Every window down Main Street had a massive X made of tape. A few stores were covered in blue tarps, where fine shards of glass shimmered in the late afternoon sunlight.

'Did Karen and the kids get reunited with their dad?'

'Oh yeah, and he got a tongue-lashing too,' replied Marcus. 'Do you want me to drive past the Inn?'

'No. Take me to the food first.' She needed something decent in her stomach, considering all she'd eaten today were candy canes.

People were everywhere. It was as if the entire town was out to party, as Marcus steered through scattered crowds of people to the main intersection where music blared from speakers set up in the pub's bottle shop. The smell of barbecued meats, fried onions and coffee filled the air, along with the sounds of children's laughter. A group of all ages played a game of Christmas street cricket near the train station, where Lucy had her food van set up nearby.

Even though it was hot and muggy, the summer weather didn't dampen the vibrant, happy vibe coming from the smiling crowd, eagerly catching up with each other.

It wasn't just about Christmas; it was a cyclone party and they'd all come together to celebrate the fact they were alive and had survived the storm.

It was the kind of street party Monet wanted to join in.

'Do you need me to fly later, because I think I can hear the beer calling me?'

'Can you give it an hour? We'll have all numbers accounted for by then,' Marcus said, nudging the buggy past people wandering all over the road. 'Then I'll shout you a cold carton for the help you've given me today.'

'Glad to help.'

'I'm glad you were there. We would've been stuffed without your road reports. Keep your receipts, I want you to invoice my office when this day is over.'

'No worries.' Monet didn't do it for the money, she did it because she could.

'I'm sorry about the Inn. You're insured, aren't you?'

Monet nodded. 'How bad is it?' It had looked bad from above.

'I've taped it off because it's a road hazard. I haven't had time to take a proper look yet. I miss Frank, he would've done a building inspection for me and for your insurance claim.'

Monet definitely didn't want to see it now.

They stopped on the edge of the park, thick with people, where Marcus got held up by others eager for news of friends and loved ones.

Monet weaved her way through the crowd, jumped the train tracks and headed for the shiny coffee van. 'Hey, Lucy, Lizzie,' she said to the mother and daughter team busily serving coffee and cake for everyone.

'*Monet!*' Lucy jumped down from the side door of her food van to envelop Monet in hug. 'I'm so sorry about the Inn. Dad's going to see what he can do, but he's been busy clearing roads.'

'It's okay, that's tomorrow's problem. What I'd love is one of your black coffees, thick enough to make the spoon stand.'

'Done. Double espresso coming right up. Food?'

'Whatever you think. Oh, I think Marcus and Mickey will need a coffee too.' She leaned against the side of the van in the shade and did a rare thing in the remote outback town—she people watched. They were everywhere.

Kids played on the vintage train they'd found beside a billabong. Parents sat on outdoor tables, under the shade of enormous beach umbrellas, while more people milled inside the tea house museum.

The crowd spilled over to the small park and into the main intersection in front of the pub. There, big Jimmy—the Caveman—stood head and shoulders above everyone, twirling his cooking tongs, manning four barbecues as he yakked to the men standing around with beers in hand.

She was really starting to develop a thirst for a beer, watching patrons cruising in and out of the pub as its jukebox cranked out the tunes. 'The publican and her staff wouldn't be too happy about missing their day off.'

'Samantha's been amazing,' replied Lucy, working away on her classy coffee machine. 'She opened her doors at dawn, offering showers for people, rooms and whatever else they can. Women and children have the rooms, the men get to sleep where they can, but everyone's offering their couches or spare rooms to keep families together. You can come stay with me. Jax and I have plenty of room.'

'Um, thanks. I hadn't thought that far.' Where was she going to sleep? Which was a rare thing, because she was so used to telling everyone there was always room to sleep at the Unofficial Elsie Creek Inn. Her heart squeezed against the empty ache of something so big missing from her life. She really didn't want to think about it. 'Have you been brewing coffee all day?'

'I have. The pub has been sharing their stashes with me to keep the coffee flowing. The publican got Jax to fetch their barbecues for the Caveman to cook on. He is such a legend, that man hasn't stopped barbecuing all day.'

'He does that.' The last barbecue she'd seen the Caveman cook at was out the back of the Inn, which went for days as part of their last cyclone clean-up party. Why was it so hard to stop thinking about the Inn?

Instead she focused on the crowd. Many were seated on blankets or camping chairs or at tables filled with plates of salad, seafood, roasted meats and snags, with plenty of servings of plum puddings and pavlova. It looked like everyone was tucking into a huge feast—she was famished. 'Where's all the food coming from?'

'Everyone,' replied Lucy. 'They're all bringing in their food because their fridges aren't working.'

'Still no power?'

Lucy shook her head. 'Who knows when they'll have town power running? We've heard there's quite a few towns without power. Marcus is telling everyone to conserve their generator fuel until Kyle can get a fuel truck in—if they can get past the flood waters. If they can't, Jax said he can get the Air Force to do a fuel drop for us.'

'The new fire chief will be a hero if he does that.'

'He's my hero every single day,' said Lucy in a love-sick swoon.

Monet smiled at how happy and in love her friend was. 'So, they're having a town Christmas lunch?' A meal she'd managed to avoid for decades—but now it surrounded her.

'Absolutely. Everyone's brought in their Christmas meals to share. If you want some salads or anything else in the way of food, you'll find it all in the tea house dining room. The old tea house kitchen is now an op shop, so if you need any clothes or bedding, help yourself. It's all free. Oh, guess what?' Lucy said, passing a mega-sized cup of coffee to Monet.

'What? And thank you. What do I owe you?'

'Nothing—they're gifts, all this food and clothing are gifts. So, Merry Christmas.'

Monet tried to smile, she really did—but it came out more like a grimace.

'I know,' said Lucy, full of Christmas cheer. 'Did you hear the Flynn brothers' movie night is finally happening?' Lucy pointed to the train station roof where a group of men were erecting a massive white screen to face the lawns. It was a good spot.

'No way, after all these years, its finally happening?' The twins, who ran the local hardware store, were like politicians chasing votes, but on movie choices. One of them wanted arty movies with subtitles, the other brother only wanted action flicks. They'd never been able to agree between them which movie to have, causing a debate that had been going on for years. 'How did the Flynn brothers agree to the movies?

'Karma, the croc, picked the movies so there's no arguing between the brothers.'

'I'll be in on that.' Although, with the weight of tiredness creeping into her bones, she'd probably be asleep before the mid-point of the first movie.

Cecil, the water buffalo, came into view. It was impossible to miss the beefy buffalo wearing bright red tinsel around his horns. Gone was the slouchy Santa hat she'd seen him wearing only a few days ago. Instead of being a vagrant wanderer, today Cecil's coat shone, being led by his owner, Esther.

In her ball gown and gumboots, Esther looked like the fairy godfarmer, leading a line of children covered in face paint that did nothing to hide their wide smiles. The children skipped, hopped, and danced in different coloured tutus in an uncoordinated conga line, following the buffalo on a tour of the tiny town park.

Monet was tempted to join that queue of dancing children.

Sipping her coffee as she scanned the crowd, it didn't take long to spot him—Mr Timothy Kirby, the Posh Prince. With beer in hand and a smile on his dial, he talked to the other men milling around the park's statue. They all wore matching wide brim hats, muddy jeans, long-sleeved shirts and deep tans.

It was the old Tim she remembered.

Did she dare say hello?

Would they ever be able to get past the awkward?

Did she dare hope he'd rush toward her and hug her like a friend and lover, the way Alex, who stood next to him, had his arm around Verily. Would Tim do that with her?

'*Tim!*' A female voice cried out.

Monet frowned at the flash of tight, blonde curls, shiny shirt and fancy cowboy boots.

Oh no. Who allowed that witch to sneak into town?

It was Sherice. The shiny, cheating Sherice. Hugging Tim. *Her* Tim!

It hurt.

Monet found it hard to swallow, forcing down the hot coffee that seared her throat. But it was numb compared to the feeling of her heart dropping like a mirror, smashing all over her boots in the perfect marriage of part anxiety and part panic attack.

But it wasn't just Tim hugging Sherice—the woman he was meant to marry in a toxic one-sided love affair—that hurt. It's what stood behind him…

With tunnel vision, all she saw was the Unofficial Elsie Creek Inn.

Monet walked straight past people who tried to talk to her. She didn't hear them. She didn't see them. She saw only the Inn.

Ducking under the police tape, her breath hitched as she stared wide-eyed at the massive tree laying on its side.

It was like a meteorite blast site.

The root ball was exposed at the base of the trunk that towered over her and it was as long and wide as a road train, made of wood and covered in bark. It left a deep gaping hole of torn roots, exposing the cracked core of a tree that had been standing longer than this town.

Her hand let go of her coffee and it splattered wide across the dirt. She didn't care.

With trembling fingertips, she touched the coarse bark as her vision blurred with tears. Her knees gave way and she crouched down beside it, cupping her mouth to stop her cries.

Her tree. Her house. Gone.

Everything was smashed like a bomb had exploded above it.

Shattered glass from the broken louvres lay everywhere. The kettle, coffee tins, and broken cups were flung near the fence line. The rattly old fridge was on its side and had lost its door. Walls were smashed flat and the raised floor had broken into a million pieces, exposing the sturdy supporting beams.

The Inn had been annihilated.

What the hell did she do that was so wrong to deserve this kind of a Christmas present, for the second time in her life?

Santa, you suck!

SEVENTEEN

Tim stood beside Alex and Verily in the shade near the small-town statue. It gave him the perfect view of both the airstrip entrance and the Unofficial Elsie Creek Inn, where he'd been keeping an eye out for Monet.

He'd seen the Inn. It hurt to see it in that condition. It was going to break Monet's heart. He didn't want her to see it on her own and didn't care what Marcus thought, he wanted to be there for Monet.

'Tim!'

He froze, recognising the voice.

Before he could bolt, his face was smothered by tight blonde curls, thick with hairspray or whatever women used. He knew who it was, instantly. 'Sherice?'

'I've been so worried about you, sugar.'

'How did you get in here?' All of the roads into town, in all directions, were flooded, creating an exclusive party for Elsie Creek residents only.

'I got a seat on the boat they're using to ferry the miners across the highway. You should've seen it, sugar. There's a heap of men eager to get back to meet their families. Although, I reckon most were keen to get to the pub. Wow, what a turnout.'

'Huh?' He readjusted his hat, stunned she was here.

Tim stood in muddy jeans and workwear like the other men who'd been clearing roads and pulling bogged cars out of ditches.

Unlike Sherice in her shiny shirt that was unbuttoned low enough to show off the lace of her pink bra. Polished cowboy boots poked out from beneath her denim bootlegs topped with a shiny belt buckle. With the perfect manicure and makeup, Sherice was all dressed up as if she were going out to dinner. He used to like that about her. She never had a hair out of place with this perfect polish to her. A look his mother had approved of.

Oh, hell. NO.

He stepped back from the ice blonde in cowboy boots, but Sherice only came closer.

'Stop, right there.'

'I've been so worried about, sugar.'

'So you've said already.' It was like a broken vinyl—as Monet would say, *long past its use-by-date.*

'You won't answer your phone.'

'It was unplugged,' butted in Alex.

Sherice sneered. 'No doubt by that Monet and her sticky fingers being where they don't belong.'

'I did it because I didn't want to talk to you.'

'But—but, sugar,' Sherice crooned in that voice that used to make him bend to her every demand. Now, it sickened him that he'd given in to this thing who'd stomped all over him and broken his trust.

'*Alex*,' called one of their neighbours, rushing towards them.

'Jasper, what's up, mate?'

'I've got to get home. How much for you to take me in your truck across the river to get me home.'

'Sorry, mate, the rivers are up too high, even for me.'

Jasper gripped at his hair, the panic obvious to everyone. 'My kid. My wife—'

'Well, you should've thought about that before you left them behind on Christmas Day,' chided Sherice.

'Don't you think I'm kicking myself enough already?' Jasper kicked the heel of his steel cap boots on the concrete. Hoisting his backpack higher up his shoulder, with his miner's hard hat clipped to the side.

'Look, Marcus is over there,' Verily said with her pronounced American accent, pointing to the beefy cop. 'Marcus might be able to help you, Jasper.'

Marcus's shoulders and arms had gotten bigger since Tim had last seen his fishing friend. Did he work out all day?

'Come on, I'll take you. The air's a lot fresher over there,' said Verily, giving Sherice a side-sneer.

'I'm coming too,' said Alex, rushing to hold Verily's hand.

That left Tim stuck with Sherice. *Great!*

'Sugar, you want me to get you some food? Drinks?'

'I want you to leave me alone.'

'But—'

'We're done.'

'But it's Christmas.'

'I've been telling you to leave me alone for months.'

'But, it's Christmas Day, sugar.'

'Don't care. I can't trust you. I'll never be able to trust you again,' he said, taking a long look at her from top to bottom. He felt nothing for her. Nothing. 'I have no idea what possessed me to date you in the first place.'

'Your mother said we'd be perfect together.'

Tim wanted to throw up. Set up by his bloody matchmaking mother.

He turned away from her. 'Have a nice life, Sherice, because we're finished.'

She reached for his arm, he flung it away.

'But you can't!'

He could, and he did.

But his getaway was cut short by Esther in her ball gown and gumboots, leading her pet water buffalo, Cecil. Right behind his big waddling butt was a group of tiny kids skipping in a parade of assorted tutus. He'd never seen so many tutus, worn by both girls and boys.

But they'd trapped him with Sherice and her perfume cloud crowding his space.

'Does anyone know what this statue is about?' Esther asked the children, who called out names or characters from some cartoon. 'This is Elsie Creek's tribute to our very own outback Mary Poppins. Many called her the Lady Mary and some called her Grandma Mary.'

Tim, with his back to the pub and the Inn, stared at the statue. Grandma Mary was Monet's grandmother. Which brought him back to his main concern: where *was* Monet?

EIGHTEEN

'You know, I put this thing up called police tape, to keep people out,' Marcus said from behind the steering wheel of the golf buggy. He was parked at the edge of the fallen tree that had completely drowned the Unofficial Elsie Creek Inn in leaves and branches.

'Yeah, well, I'm allergic to rules, Sarge.' Monet stood, wiping her tears. She didn't even know she'd been crying. She hated crying and slipped on her aviators to shield her eyes.

There was nothing salvageable under the tree.

The poor tree.

She'd loved this tree, enjoying its shade as part of her Sunday ritual for years. 'Where are my slippers?'

'Your what?'

'My red sparkly shoes.'

Marcus looked at her like she was nuts—and she was.

'Didn't you see *The Wizard of Oz*?'

Marcus screwed his nose up.

'Oh, come on, it's a classic. There's a huge storm making a house land on the wicked witch who is wearing red sparkly tap-dancing shoes.' Monet pointed to the tree that covered her house with her voice rising with the strain. 'As this town's *Wicked Witch of the Westerly Winds*, where are *my freaking red shiny shoes!*'

'I'm so sorry,' said Marcus.

She took a deep shaky breath. 'Not your fault.' It was no one's fault. 'What's up?'

'Jasper's wife and son are trapped on their property, Bonny Plains. Do you know the place?'

'I do. It's been a while.' Monet stepped over branches, broken glass, and splintered wood to get to Marcus. Each step fracturing her soul.

She pushed it way down, kicking those emotions into a trunk she'd lock into a concrete bunker to forget about, and focused on Marcus, the man in charge of everyone's safety. 'We don't have Bonny Plains on our station sheet, it's vacant.'

'Not anymore. Are you up for a flight?'

'Sure.' She'd rather hang in the air with Gertrude and blast her tunes, screaming out a lungful of sadness than be here.

'The only problem is...' Marcus removed his dark

shades and rubbed his tired eyes.

'Yeah?'

'She's pregnant. Isn't there some unwritten rule about carrying pregnant passengers?'

'What?' Her heart squeezed ice through her veins as she stopped mid-stride. 'Why did Jasper leave her out there?'

'The mine called them in to do a clean-up assessment. They weren't expecting the flooding to be so swift, or this severe. His wife told him to go, to help pay for the renovations. Believe me, Jasper is a wreck over it.'

'How far gone is she?'

'Jasper's in such a flap he can't remember if it's seven or eight months. I'm waiting for the doctor to let me know?'

'The hot doc or his dad?'

'Doc Senior is out of range, checking on the communities. Stewart's in surgery fixing the boy you brought in. The one with the broken arm.'

'Well, I'm not leaving a mother and child out there on their own.'

'I was hoping you'd say that. I'm sure the lady will fill you in when you meet her. Here,' he said, handing her a cup of coffee. 'I saw you drop yours. When this is all over, I'll buy you a bottle of tequila to go with that beer. We'll drink it out the back of the station with our feet up, looking at Gertrude on the runway.'

'At the risk of ruining my reputation by being seen drinking with local constabulary in public, you're on.' She climbed into the spare seat of the tricked-up golf cart and let it whisk her away, and she didn't look back.

Her past was done.

Tim was done, he had his Shiny Sherice. Monet had Gertrude.

All she could do was keep her eyes on the sky ahead, and get through this nightmare of a day.

NINETEEN

'Tim, I'm trying to talk to you!' Sherice whined, tugging on his arm as they stood in the town's park near the bronze statue of a boy.

'Shh, I'm listening to Esther.' Tim nodded to a few locals who had also gathered to listen to the lady.

The octogenarian, wearing glittery face paint of a butterfly, smiled at him. Esther used to be Tim's art teacher, now long-retired, but he had always loved her stories as a kid.

'Now, does anyone know why they called Grandma Mary the outback's Mary Poppins?' Esther asked the children as she patted the hind of her pet water buffalo.

'Mary Poppins? Did she have a brolly like Aunty Molly?' asked one of Karen's kids. All of them wore face paint that sparkled in the late afternoon sun.

'Better… a plane,' said Esther. 'Mary was a pilot in an around-the-world air race that started in Canada, went through Europe, then Asia and was meant to end in Melbourne. But there was a horrendous dust storm when Mary left Darwin, heading to Adelaide, and she lost her bearings. The red dust filled her plane and clogged her engine, forcing her to land in the middle of nowhere.'

The kids gasped, with necks craned back as they sat on the lawn while Cecil the buffalo, chewed the grass around the statue.

Esther had everyone's attention. She wasn't hard to miss with her sparkly ball gown, standing in the middle of the children like a retired fairy godmother without wings.

Esther continued, 'Stranded in the outback, under the searing sun, Mary's plane wouldn't start. She saw no houses, no people, only flat red soil, and the dirt track. Mary was lost, so she waited in the shade of the wings until it was cool enough to fix her plane. Then, just as she thought all hope was lost, a truck rattled in the distance, shimmering with the heat waves that rose under the sun. Mary thought it was a mirage.'

'Was it real?' One of the children asked.

'It was. It was a truck driven by a strapping young man named Noel. Nibbsy, to his friends. He was a fettler with the railway company.'

'What's a fettler?' asked various children.

'A fettler is someone who looks after the railway lines so they're safe for the trains to ride on.' Esther then patted her heart and sighed as she said, 'Oh, and it was love at first sight as he towed what he called the angel from the skies, and her plane, back to Elsie Creek. But when Mary arrived in town, she caused quite a stir, because she was a proper lady with a plane.'

'Why?' asked the little girl, screwing up her freckly nose.

'The plucky Mary had lied to get into a strictly men's-only air race. That's why she'd dressed herself up to look like a man.' Esther patted the statue that looked like a boy in vintage aviator's clothing.

Tim blinked, only realising now, on closer inspection, it was a woman. Some of the others around him also murmured their surprise.

'When Mary's family found out what she had done, they were outraged,' said Esther. 'Telegrams were flying backwards and forwards to the Lady Mary, who was a distant relative to the Queen of England.'

'Nooo,' gushed the children, along with a few of the adults.

'It's true. The Lady Mary caused even more of a scandal because she fell in love with and married a commoner, the fettler, Nibbsy. And for a wedding present, the poms from her side of the world disowned Mary, but the town didn't. They made her our very own ten-pound pom. And it was Mary and Nibbsy who built the Unofficial Elsie Creek Inn.' Esther pointed, with sadness in her eyes at the house destroyed by the tree.

'Why do they call it the Unofffff—' The little girl with the missing front teeth stammered with the word.

'The Unofficial Elsie Creek Inn earned its name because it became a boarding house for station kids,' replied Esther. 'It was before the School of the Air and long before today's technology was available in the Territory. Mary would fly around collecting all the station kids for school. Even if those families couldn't afford it, Mary would look after those children during school terms where they'd stay at the Unofficial Elsie Creek Inn. Then she'd fly them home for the holidays when the school term was finished.' Esther then pointed to the train station, and the children's heads swivelled. 'It was also a common sight to see Mary carting a load of books in a wheelbarrow. She shared them with stockmen, even the soldiers stationed here after the war. Mary taught many men to read while they waited for the train, that's how that bench seat got made. The station's platform and that bench seat were Mary's classroom.'

The kids swivelled to stare at the chair in the platform's shade. Many in town knew it as the part-time shelter for Homeless Hank, who wasn't homeless anymore.

Alex mumbled next to Tim, 'I always wondered why that seat was there.'

Tim nodded.

'Mary loved to read,' continued Esther. 'She'd read to

all those who stayed at the Inn.'

'Why is it called an inn when it's just a house?' called out a boy.

'Because the children who first stayed there didn't like the name boarding house, they enjoyed being called guests at the Inn. That's why they called it the *Unofficial Elsie Creek Inn*. It made all of those children feel special, even if they slept on the floor.'

'Why the floor?' Asked another one of the little boys.

'Because the Unofficial Elsie Creek Inn never had air-conditioning. Everyone knew the coolest place to sleep was in the lounge. If you got under the ceiling fans beside the walls of louvres, that's where the cool breeze flowed through. And, you know what?' Esther said, smiling at Tim and Alex among a group of men who had also stopped to listen. 'All those little boys and girls who were as small as you, grew up, and they still sleep on the floor of the Inn whenever they're in town because the Inn's new owner never closed her doors to anyone.'

'Where is the new owner?' asked a little girl.

At that moment, music carried from the plane with the broomstick painted on its underbelly, zooming high above them.

'That's her,' said Esther, and they all craned their necks to the sky holding the little red plane. 'That's Mary's granddaughter, Monet. Doing just what her grandmother used to do, bringing all the children into town. That beautiful, mischievous girl is working really hard to keep families together, especially on Christmas Day.' Esther smiled down at the children and said, 'And I know Grandma Mary would have loved to see you all here today. So, how about we all use that chalk you've got to draw some pictures of Monet or Mary and their planes on the paths around the statue?'

Tim frowned at the red plane getting smaller and smaller in a vast blue sky. It ticked him off, he'd missed her. How did that happen?

He frowned harder at the shiny bottle blonde next to him. She wasn't the blonde he wanted. 'We're over. Forever.'

He turned his back on Sherice, forgetting all about her. His ex-fiancée didn't matter to him and he'd wasted too much time on that trash.

When he again saw the Unofficial Elsie Creek Inn smothered by the tree, it made his guts squeeze tight. It would have crushed Monet to see it like that.

He'd forgotten about the Inn's history, now remembering what it had meant to him too.

Even though Tim was determined to wait for Monet, to talk to her about last night, and to find out what Marcus meant to her, he also couldn't stand around and wait any longer. 'I'm getting my chainsaw,' he said to Alex. 'Can you bring your truck around and we'll organise some utes and clear the tree, to at least get into the Inn and see the damage.'

Word soon spread and more men stepped out of the

pub, putting their beers down and sliding on their Akubras as they came from all over to gather in front of the Inn. With Tim taking charge, the clean-up began.

They all owed Mary.

They all owed Monet.

Because they'd all been boarders at the Unofficial Elsie Creek Inn that stood no more.

It had been a home away from home… for all of them.

TWENTY

Monet circled above the tiny house on the hill, surrounded by a sea of water. A small boy vigorously waved at her with a border collie bounding beside him, as a woman stepped off the porch.

Monet had tried to radio them, but there was no answer. Had they lost power?

She scoured for a place to land.

The choices she had were a spindly track, or the paddock.

She swooped low over the dirt road filled with large jagged rocks and deep corrugations. It was a jawbreaker. Nearer to the house, guarding a cattle grid, was a fence that was tough enough to knock the wings off her plane.

That left the paddock on the other side of the hill.

There was no livestock, but the water was rising, and the sun was sinking. She hadn't realised it was so late in the day.

Yet, there was still enough time to land, bundle up the family and leave.

Monet made another pass and took her shot, coming in low. She kept her eyes on the green patchy weeds that carpeted the red shoaly dirt, hoping Gertrude's struts held on. This was going to be rough.

The plane touched down, bounced high, then down again.

'Come on Gertrude, it's just a hill.' Monet wrestled with the controls as they careened over the uneven terrain. One of the plane's legs smashed into an ant mound sending red powdery mud and dust into the sky. The plane jerked hard all the way to her shoulders as she held on with gritted teeth. She adjusted the flaps in fear of spinning, and again the plane bounced up, then slammed back down to earth. Each landing was a jolt to her spine. But she had to do this. They were going to do this. And now.

Putting everything into it, she gripped the steering tight and held her breath as the water line came rushing towards her. They were running out of space to slow down. This is where her boat anchor would come in handy to toss out behind her.

Finally, they landed and slowed to a stop.

Monet's entire body was tense. Her arms and

shoulders ached from gripping the yoke, she trembled as the sweat made her shirt stick to her skin.

If Mickey had seen that landing, he would have screamed at her, then grounded her, taking away her keys to Gertrude forever.

'Thank you, Gertrude. I wouldn't have put you through this if I didn't have to.' She patted the plane's dash in the cockpit. 'Elsie Creek Tower, this is Double W One. Over,' she said into the microphone.

'Elsie Creek Tower here. Go ahead, kid,' came Mickey's gruff voice over the speakers.

'I've landed at Bonny Plains. I'll radio when I take off.'

'Good. Make it snappy, kid, it's beer o'clock.'

'Don't I know it. Over and out.'

She climbed out of the plane as the cool fresh air washed over her. She was greeted at the door by a small boy and his dog. 'Hi there, what's your name?'

'Brendan. What's yours?'

'Monet. Is this your dog?' Always prepared, she pulled out the dog treats she kept on board, because stations always had a dog on duty. Mind you, her stash was getting low after the trips she'd done today, but she tossed more treats to the dog.

'That's Bomber. He's named after Dad's favourite footy club. Have you seen my daddy?'

'I have. It was your dad who sent me out here to collect you guys.'

'He did!' The kid's eyes lit up like a freaking Christmas tree, it was like a shot to the heart. It made her risky landing so worth it. 'Where's your mum?'

'In the house,' said little Brendan, grabbing her hand. He dragged her down the tiny hill with Bomber bounding beside them. 'Her tummy hurts. Does that mean the baby's coming?'

Oh, no. The hairs on the back of her neck bristled.

A woman waited by the wire gates that surrounded their flourishing garden. A four-wheel-drive was parked under the nearby carport. The house seemed freshly painted, with new solar panels running along the roof. Building materials for more renovations were strapped down nearby.

'Hi, I'm Monet. Jasper sent me.'

'I'm Chrissie. Thank you for coming.' The woman, with the big baby bump, hugged Monet.

It was a really big belly.

Chrissie winced, gripping her lower back. 'Sorry, the Braxton Hicks have been killing me.'

'All day,' piped in the little boy.

Monet gazed at Chrissie with widening eyes. 'Are you sure its Braxton Hicks? How far along are you?'

'Are you worried about taking me on the plane?'

'No. Not at all. It's your choice. Just don't go into labour while we're in the air.' But they didn't have a moment to waste. 'So, let's do this.'

Monet crouched down so she could speak to the little

boy at eye level. 'Brendan, how about you go and grab your favourite toy and a bag of clothes for a sleepover?' She pointed to the toy by the side of the house. 'You can use that red trolley to start dragging gear to the plane for me. You'll be a proper baggage handler like they have at the airports.'

His eyes widened with excitement. 'Are we going for a ride?'

'We are, but first I need to talk to your mummy, okay?'

Brendan eagerly ran into the house with his dog bounding after him.

Monet stood and faced Chrissie. 'How far along are you?'

'Eight and a half months.'

Shiiiiiiiiiit. Monet wiped over her mouth. 'We can do this.'

Chrissie gave a deep guttural groan as she bent over with trembling legs. 'Oh, no,' she cried, panting for air with eyelids shut tight.

A liquid trickled between Chrissie's legs. Crouching over so low, she almost toppled over Monet had to hold the woman up.

'What's wrong with Mummy?' Brendan cried from the doorway.

'You're right, mate, the baby is coming.' Monet tried to swallow the fear rising in her throat. She'd delivered cattle, horses, dogs, even kittens. She'd babysat bunches of turtle, chickens and crocodile eggs, but never a newborn human baby before. 'Let's get you in the house.'

Inside the open-plan house the heat hit Monet as her eyes adjusted. The ceiling fans were as still as the decorations that covered the Christmas tree. Assorted Christmas cards lined the bookcase and hand-drawn pictures of Santa and his elves covered the fridge, surrounded by an assortment of eskies.

Chrissie sat awkwardly on a dining chair, clutching the edge of the kitchen table with a white-knuckle grip.

'What happened to your power?' Monet grabbed a tea towel she soaked under the running tap, then splashed water over her own face. She passed the wet cloth and water bottle to Chrissie.

'We had town power until last night. Jasper was collecting fuel for the generator from work.' Chrissie exhaled slowly, exercising some Lamaze technique to control the pain.

It looked freaking painful to Monet.

'Mum said we should have had enough sunshine for the solar to charge the batteries,' piped in Brendan. 'But they broke from last night's scary storm.'

'Well, okay then. Brendan, you pack a bag and keep your mum company, I've got to use the radio in the plane. I'll be right back.' Monet bolted out the door, sprinting to her plane as fast as she could.

Scrambling into her seat, she gasped to catch her breath. Through the cockpit's window, the water glistened like diamonds under the late afternoon sun. It had risen heaps in the short time she'd been here, swallowing the land around the hill.

How long did they have before they ran out of dry land to leave?

'Elsie Creek Hospital, Elsie Creek Hospital. This is Double W One, over.' Her voice may have sounded calm but her heart rate hammered in her ears.

'This is Elsie Creek Hospital,' came the reply through the speakers. 'Go ahead, Double W One?'

'I'm at Bonny Plains Station and have a pregnant woman. Her water has broken and she's in labour, as we speak.'

'Um… Um…

'Who is this?'

'I'm the receptionist, the rest are all busy—'

'Find me a midwife. I'm about to get flooded in. THIS IS AN EMERGENCY.' People had thrown those words around all day, saying it was life and death. *Nah-ah.* They were only practice runs. This was the real deal.

Monet licked her dry lips, tasting the salt from her sweat mixing with the metallic flavour of fear in the back of her throat. She sculled from her warm water bottle as an errant sweat bead trickled from her hairline to sting her eyes.

The seconds seemed to stretch into hours she didn't have to waste, as she willed the radio to speak.

'Double W One, this is Head Nurse of the Elsie Creek Hospital. Over.'

Finally. 'Jenny. It's Monet.'

Jenny, their new head nurse was a magical midwife.

'Hey, Monet, Merry Christmas.'

Whatever! There was nothing bloody merry about today. 'I'm at Bonny Plains with Chrissie, whose water just broke, and she's having contractions. Painful ones. What do I do?'

'Get her comfortable—you may be there for a while. Can we send an ambulance?'

'No can do. I need to fly her out of here asap. The floodwaters are rising as we speak. Can she fly?' Monet eyed the water line that was getting far too close for her liking. Having flown over the floodwaters all day, she'd seen the man-eating crocodiles reach new territories to hunt. Her skin prickled and her scalp tingled as sweat ran cold down her spine as all those scary childhood stories of the Billabong Bunyip started to haunt her.

'And have a baby on the plane?' Jenny asked.

'Can. She. Fly?'

'I'd say no, wait for the baby. Look, ask the mother, it's her decision to make.'

'I will. I'll be right back. Over.' Monet tossed the handpiece onto her pilot's seat and dashed back down the hill.

Chrissie's deep painful moaning echoed out of the house.

Poor little Brendan stood by the front door with a worried expression, hugging his teddy bear tightly.

'It'll be okay, mate. Do me a favour?'

He looked up at Monet with enormous eyes, doing his best to be brave, giving her a nod.

'Can you get your dog's lead and bowl for me? Put them in your little red wagon and take them up to the plane. I'll make you my co-pilot.'

'Wow. A co-pilot. Cool.'

She ruffled the little boy's hair and stepped inside the house. 'Chrissie, we have a choice. We stay and hopefully the floods won't rise any higher, or we move to the plane now.'

Chrissie was standing over the table, gripping its edges, drenched in sweat. 'Plane. We take the plane.'

'Excellent choice. Being this close to birth you'd have a bag packed, already? Somewhere?' Monet hoped.

'In the car.'

'I'll drive the car around and pick you up.' Monet swiped the keys off the counter. In the family car, she reversed out of the carport and drove it as close to the front door as she could.

Brendan came running down the hill from the plane. 'You drove over Mummy's flowers?'

'Sorry, mate, I'll replace them later.'

'It's okay, Brendan,' said Chrissie, holding onto the door frame.

Monet bounded up the steps to meet her. 'We need sheets and towels, mate, can you grab them for me?'

Brendan ran into the house as Monet helped Chrissie

into the car.

'Monet,' Chrissie said, grabbing her hand from the passenger seat. 'The floodwaters are rising, aren't they?'

'People pay me for brutal honesty—so, do you want me to answer that or ignore your question?'

'Tell me.'

'They're rising. And if I don't get us out of here in the next hour, I won't have enough room for a take-off. Then we'll be having a roof party.' Where she'd strip down Gertrude's spotlights and batteries, load up her shotgun and flares, to play patrol guard all night watching out for any lurking man-eating predators that liked to sneak up on you in the dark.

If, and when they made it back to town, Monet was definitely ordering some amphibian floats to extend Gertrude's wardrobe.

'We go. Now.'

'*Thank you.*' Monet smiled at the woman. Determined and tough.

After getting the mother settled in her seat, Monet ran inside to check on the boy. She spotted a handbag she assumed was Chrissie's. 'Chrissie, where's your cyclone kit with all your papers?' Everyone had one somewhere, especially after last night.

'In the bathroom.' She called from the front seat.

Monet carried out the plastic box.

Brendan followed, dragging out a towering pile of sheets and towels they dumped into the car.

Locking the house behind her, Monet bundled up the boy and his dog into the back. With the moaning mother in the passenger seat, Monet drove them up the hill to the waiting plane.

'You sit on the stairs, Chrissie, it's cooler there than inside the plane. I'll load up and return the car to clear my flight path. Okay?'

'Okay, okay.' Again, Chrissie winced. The contractions were coming quicker and stronger.

Monet had to get the car out of the way, so she tore down the hill and parked it. She then ran back up the hill with heavy legs. 'I've gotta do more cardio.'

Only to come face to face with the mother.

It was a hellish look. Chrissie's red cheeks were forcing out the air as her groans deepened. Her arms trembled, with a white-knuckle grip on either side of the door where she had planted herself, spread-legged on the steps of the plane.

'It's coming. NOW.'

'Oh, hell no.' *Why now?* Monet dragged the muggy still air deep into her lungs and looked to the sky for an answer. Something. 'Brendan, get on the radio.'

'I don't know how to use a radio?'

'The handpiece is on my seat.' She lifted the kid over his mother and into the plane, then pointed toward the cockpit. 'Pick it up and push down the button on the side. Speak into it and say, Elsie Creek Hospital this is Double W One, over. Then let go of the button.'

The little boy did as she'd instructed.

'This is Elsie Creek Hospital, who is this?' replied Jenny, loud and clear over the speakers.

'Brendan, can you hold down the button for me and I'll shout?' Monet asked.

'Like this?' He held up the handpiece.

'Jenny, can you hear me? Over.' Monet then said to Brendan, 'When I say *over*, you let go of the button, okay?'

And he did.

'I can,' replied Jenny.

She nodded to Brendan who pushed down the button for her, holding up the microphone like a journalist at a press conference.

'Jenny, Chrissie's crowning. The baby is definitely in a rush to get out. What the hell do I do? Oh, and we're doing this via passenger relay. Just tell me what to do and I'll do everything you say. Over.'

Brendan let go of the button with a grin.

Monet wiped her sweaty face on her clammy T-shirt. She winked at the boy, pretending to be calm when she was on the verge of a full-blown panic attack.

Jenny's voice carried over the speakers. 'Okay, crash course in midwifery. Chrissie is a healthy woman. It's not her first baby, she'll know what to do.'

Monet looked to Chrissie. 'Do you hear that?'

Sweat plastered over Chrissie's forehead, which Monet wiped away with a towel.

'We can do this. I'm here to help you, Chrissie. Just

tell me what you need?'

Chrissie could only nod, breathing hard, with a trembling grip on the sides of the open door of the plane.

And as Jenny calmly coached them over the radio, Monet remained beside Chrissie. The mother's teeth-clenched screams echoed over the valley as the sun started to sink and the floodwaters continued to rise.

TWENTY-ONE

Tim frowned hard at the cracked concrete of the Unofficial Elsie Creek Inn's driveway, listening to the speakers on the open doors of Alex's truck. Every vehicle in the vicinity with a two-way radio echoed the sound of Monet's voice.

Tim had heard Monet's fear straight away; it spiked pure ice through his veins.

'Jenny, Chrissie's crowning,' Monet's voice carried over the two-way speakers. 'The baby is definitely in a rush to get out. What the hell do I do?'

Jenny, their bush hospital's head nurse, replied over the speakers. 'Okay, crash course in midwifery…'

Tim swallowed hard and bolted for the airport. Mickey would be listening. So too would the town's top cop, Marcus. Both men would know where Monet was.

'Marcus, where is Monet?' Tim asked, barrelling into the airport hangar's office.

Marcus was leaning his hip against the large reception counter, arms crossed over his barrel chest with his head down, listening intently.

On the opposite side was Mickey, resting his ruddy chin on two hands with elbows on the bench, keeping an ear close to the large two-way radio.

This was Elsie Creek's airport office, which stood directly beneath the radio control tower where the radio signal was as powerful as it would ever get. And Mickey was known for always listening in to the airwaves.

'She's at Jasper's, Bonny Plains,' said Marcus, pointing back to Jasper jerkily pacing over by the far wall.

'She's early,' said Jasper, chewing his nails as he paced back and forth. 'Chrissie's not meant to have the baby for another few weeks.'

'The baby's all healthy?' Tim asked. 'The mother's passed all the tests and stuff?'

'Yeah. Yeah. Chrissie's just early.'

'Stress, mate. It's been a stressful couple of days for everyone,' said Mickey, the worry deepening the crevices around his eyes.

'You're telling me,' said Marcus.

'Hey, have you got an airstrip out there?' Mickey asked Jasper, who shrugged.

'We only moved in a few months ago. It was pretty

run-down and we've only been working on the house.'

'That's why you're not on the station's register,' said Marcus. 'Mickey, draw them one of those mud maps.'

'Gawd, what did that kid land on? Nope, don't tell me.' Mickey stole some paper from the fax machine. Bitching under his breath, snatching up a pen, he started to draw a picture at the bench.

'What station register?' Tim asked. 'Am I on it?'

'If you've got a plane, you're not,' Marcus said.

'I sold my dad's plane. I never got my licence.'

'That Rigby Downs mob has always had special treatment from Monet, until she nicked off to Spain.' Mickey wagged his pen at Tim and said, 'I blame you for that.'

'All right, Mickey, you just draw while I explain,' said Marcus and faced the other two men. 'A few years ago, when I got the job as town sergeant, Monet approached me about starting a station register.'

'For what?' Tim asked.

'He'd tell you, if you'd zip it,' grumbled Mickey.

Marcus inhaled deeply with his chest rising, standing tall as a cop of solid muscle. He slid his thumbs into his police belt that held his gun, cuffs and pepper spray. 'Monet discovered there was a Federal Government grant available for those living in remote areas. It was for mail deliveries and to help to deliver freight in the wet season. Tess from the Post Office helped Monet set it all up.'

'So that's how Monet's been able to afford to fly

around,' said Jasper.

'Bit more than that, mate,' grizzled Mickey, scribbling on the paper, the pink tip of his tongue poking out of the corner of his mouth.

'Are you doing this register thing, for Monet, because you're dating her?' Tim blurted out. He didn't like it.

'I'm what?' Marcus asked in surprise, his face screwed up at Tim.

'You're not with Monet?' Tim asked, rubbing the back of his neck with frustrated confusion.

'Monet would rather swallow avgas than hang out with a cop after hours.' Mickey wagged his pen at Tim, saying, 'And I thought you knew the girl better than that.'

'Oi!' Marcus scowled at Mickey on the other side of the counter as he pointed to his shirt. 'What does this uniform say to you, you grumpy old bastard?'

'But the phone calls to Monet?' Tim had to know.

'I rang Monet for work,' replied Marcus.

'Monet works for the police?' Now that was a sentence Tim would never think to say.

'Monet would bitch-slap you for that,' Mickey spat out, snort-laughing spittle.

'I'll cuff you around the ear in a minute,' warned Marcus to the old man belly laughing.

'What has Monet got to do with the police?' Tim asked, pointing at the Northern Territory Police patches worn on Marcus's stocky arms.

'Monet doesn't just deliver mail, she's also a trained

counsellor,' replied Marcus.

'Since when?' Tim looked to Marcus for answers, who turned to Mickey.

'Long time. That kid did it on account of people thinking she's crazy. She's not, but she recognises crazy or when something's wrong—'

'Monet's able to recognise the signs if someone's in distress. In your case, Jasper, postnatal depression for your wife,' finished Marcus. 'Not that I'm saying she will, but there's plenty of help available to her.'

'Monet would know all that from her mother,' Tim said.

Marcus nodded. 'Somehow that sassy bush pilot has gone and turned her sad story into a survival guide for others. Monet also discovered that if they all thought she was nuts, people opened up to her more, asking her if they were going crazy too.'

'There's nothing wrong with Monet's mental health,' Tim said firmly.

'I know that,' replied Marcus. 'Monet's been using it to get people to talk to her, and they do. Especially the men that never talk to anyone about this subject, but they'll open up to Monet.'

'Her reputation... Monet wasn't sleeping with them—'

'She was talking to them,' said Marcus decisively. 'She's been helping them out, as a mate. That's it.'

Tim was thinking of Cowboy Craig, who'd called for

Monet, when he said, 'Monet's told no one anything to protect all those ringer's reputations.' While Monet's reputation was being trashed.

Marcus nodded.

'Pfft, that kid's a freaking nun.' Again, Mickey aimed his pen at Tim. 'I blame you for that, too.'

Choosing to ignore the grumpy old man, Tim said to Marcus, 'Exactly what does Monet do to help people?' Is that what she'd been doing for Tim at the station this whole time?

'If Monet's ever worried about anyone, she'll tell me,' explained Marcus. 'I then use my powers as an officer, to have a word to the hospital. The Northern Territory, unfortunately, has the highest suicide rates in the country. What we try to do is meet once a month to ensure we leave no one out, so they never feel like they're alone. We don't get into people's business if that's what you're thinking. It's just a spreadsheet that keep tabs on our remote neighbours, with at least one confirmed sighting for shopping or at the pub per month. The dry season we don't worry so much with most of them coming to town for the musters. It's mostly during the wet season when the roads are closed off and people become isolated, that's when we keep a close eye on them.'

'Sandy...' Tim looked to both Marcus and Mickey. 'Monet was talking with Cowboy Craig about Sandlot Sandy?'

'Didn't Sandy's wife leave him?' Jasper asked.

Marcus nodded. 'Monet was worried about Sandy. We both were. So, Monet called in a favour to get Craig to take Sandy home with him for Christmas. She's also got her cousin, Rigsy, going to help Sandy for the musters.'

It all made sense now. All those phone calls to the house for Monet, the conversations with Marcus, it was a working relationship. Monet was ensuring no one suffered the way she did as a kid. Tim's respect and admiration for the woman just went through the roof.

Marcus continued. 'Sadly, Christmas is the worst time and Monet's Inn used to help out a lot, keeping tabs on people.'

'It's a damned shame what happened to the Inn,' grumbled Mickey. 'Has the kid seen it yet?'

'Yeah, I picked her up from there. She was crushed,' said Marcus.

'When did…?' Tim wiped his mouth. *Damn*, he'd missed her. 'Does Monet do the counselling stuff?' He was astounded by all the new things he'd learned about her in a few minutes, when he'd known her all his life.

'No. Monet is skilled at recognising the signs. She has a knack of making herself approachable with people, to convince them to get the help they need. She then leaves it up to the professionals,' said Marcus. 'That's when I'll take our new bush nurse, Jenny, or the doc out for a cruise. We let them think we're on a tourist tour and do medical checks, while I conduct a random firearm inspection. But it all starts with Monet, she's the unsung hero who has helped out hundreds of cattlemen, just by providing a roof and a conversation.'

'How will Monet be able to keep helping you, Marcus, if there's no more Inn?' Tim said as his heart went cold. Icy cold.

Marcus wiped over his mouth.

'She's got no reason to stay, has she?' Tim said, with that icy fear tightening its grip around his heart. 'Especially if no one had even noticed that she'd gone to Spain.' He didn't even know she'd left. Monet had a plane, she could go anywhere, anytime. And with no Inn there was nothing keeping her in Elsie Creek.

'I knew the kid went to Spain on holiday,' mumbled Mickey, head down scribbling on the paper. 'She retraced her Grandmother's flight path in that air-race Mary never finished. But Monet did. She'd send me daily emails of her trek and made me join that Instagrammy-thing to see where she was at. Then when she caught up with her mother, it was all about bloody olives and wine, yakking on about how hot the Spanish cops were.' Mickey then held out the piece of paper he'd been drawing on to Jasper. 'Here, this is for you.'

'What's this?'

'The plans for the airstrip you're gonna build.'

'What?' Jasper turned the piece of paper around like a puzzle that was too hard to solve, and looked at Marcus for answers.

'Most people use their dirt roads or keep a mowed

section of a field,' said Mickey.

'Bonny Plains used to use their main driveway,' said Tim, rubbing at his tight chest. 'I remember going there with Dad when I was a boy. We helped them build the rock levy to protect the house from the river ever rising. Is that still standing? It's a rock wall about knee height.'

'Um...' Jasper paused, scratching the back of his head. 'No. We pinched those rocks for my wife's vegetable garden.'

'And the driveway?' Tim asked.

'It's pretty rough. We were going to get it graded in the dry.'

'But it's clear, right? All the way up to the house? No new fences?' Tim asked, trying not to worry.

'We put in a boundary fence around the house to keep our son and the dog in.'

'Jeez, what the hell did that kid land on?' Mickey asked again.

'Monet would have improvised,' said Tim with supreme confidence over her skills as a pilot.

'What matters most is she's there,' said Marcus, pointing to the radio that relayed Jenny's calm voice.

'They'll wanna get a move on cos we're runnin' out of daylight and that kid don't like landing in the dark.'

'You've got runway lights, don't you?' Marcus asked Mickey.

'Used to, but the bloody dingoes chew on them like dog toys.'

'Right, well, we'd better rig something up.' Marcus stood tall, adjusting his police cap.

'We can use toilet paper rolls soaked in kerosene and line them up along the runway. We did it out home with dad a few times,' suggested Tim.

'Right you are. I've got enough packets of dunny paper stashed out the back to do the trick,' said Mickey, waddling around the reception desk toward the corridor. 'We'll need some sort of X for the kid. She doesn't land in the dark without an X marking the spot, and I haven't got enough bog rolls for that. Pity I haven't got any glow-in-the dark paint left.'

'I'm sure the Flynn brothers will have some in their hardware store, I'll go—'

'Don't waste your time, cos I know there's none in this town,' said Mickey with that familiar scowl deepening.

'How come?' Tim asked.

'Cos some bossy coppa stopped all of the town's stores from selling spray paint to try and stop that roof tagger.' Mickey gave a sly grin and a low chuckle, pointing to the police station's sloping roof through his window. 'Fat lot of good that did, eh?'

Marcus cleared his throat, wiping down the dust from his face as Tim's eyes widened at the roof of the police station. The strong arm of the law painting was massive. And clear as day.

'What's this about an X? Like marking the spot on a pirate map?' Jasper asked Tim.

'Don't stress,' he said to the worried dad-to-be, 'Monet needs something to aim for.'

'We're low on torches, batteries, and spare generators,' said Marcus.

Tim looked around the office until his eyes landed on the thick candle. It had a Christmas card attached to it saying:

Merry Christmas, Mickey.
From Tess.

Tess ran the Post Office.

The Elsie Creek Post Office was part of the town's very busy craft store.

'Didn't the women have some candle making class at the craft store?' Tim picked up the thick cathedral candle. He had the same weighty candles in his bathroom, that had been given to Monet as presents.

'They're Kat's candles,' said Marcus. 'Everyone got a Kat candle for Christmas.'

Tim pulled out his mobile and hit a number.

'Who are you calling?'

'Alex, he was standing right next to Kyle, who's married to Kat,' said Tim. 'Hello, Alex,' he said over the phone.

'Hey, where did you go? Are you hearing this drama on the radio?'

'I am, and I'm at the airport. Are Kat and Verily

nearby?'

'Yeah, they're right here. Hold on, I'll put you on speaker.'

'We're here, Tim,' said Verily with her American accent.

'We need candles. All those big ones with a glass cover, for a night landing. Can you girls do that?'

'Only one car,' called out Marcus. 'We want the airport free from people. Only one vehicle brings out that stuff, because this will be an emergency landing.'

Jasper moaned, dragging his hands down his face.

'We're onto it,' said Verily, and the call ended.

'You'd better not be planning to have any naked flames at an airport with all that avgas just sitting out there?' snapped out the beefy fireman in the doorway. The man had some serious ink covering some seriously muscular arms. 'You'll blow us all up.'

'Bull. Plenty of us mob have done it before. Anyhow, who invited you to our TP-ing party,' grumbled Mickey, coming in from the back room with his arms loaded with bags of toilet paper.

'Here, let me help you, Mickey. Where do I find the kerosene?' Tim asked, carrying a load of paper. He had to do something.

'Not on my watch, you won't,' barked out the fireman.

'You can't stop me from bringing my girl in to land,' snapped back Tim.

'I'm with Tim, that's my family in that plane too,' said Jasper, stepping in beside Tim.

'All right, fellas,' called out Marcus, playing piggie in the middle of them all. 'Let's all take a step back.'

Tim, Mickey and Jasper did, glaring at the inked fireman.

'Jax is right,' said Marcus.

'Of course, the coppa would side with the other uniform,' mumbled Mickey to Tim. 'They're sparring partners, you know. Bloody gym junkies.'

Both buffed-up men in uniform scowled at Mickey, who hid behind Tim and Jasper, hugging his toilet paper.

'Are you Lucy's Jax?' Tim asked the fireman.

'I am.'

'Huh.' Tim calmed down, catching Jasper's questioning look. 'You know Lucy, The Station Hand's daughter.'

Jasper nodded in recognition.

Tim then said to Jax, 'Well, didn't you score the scary father-in-law of the year?' And just like that, the tension was gone. Mickey chuckled and Marcus playfully patted Tim on the shoulder.

'Jax, this is Tim from Rigby Downs. That there is the new dad, Jasper from Bonny Plains,' said Marcus, as the men cordially shook hands.

'I heard. Congratulations on the incoming baby,' said Jax.

'Yeah, if we can get them to land,' said Tim.

'That's why I'm here to help, and we'll do this safely, fellas,' said Jax.

'Jax is ex-air force. He may have a trick or two,' Mickey said from the sidelines, his chin resting on an enormous plastic bag of toilet paper he hugged like a pillow. 'I still reckon we do the dunny rolls.'

The radio speakers screeched, catching their attention where a woman screamed over the two-way; it then went dead.

'Are you there, Monet?' called out Jenny. 'Anyone? This is Elsie Creek Hospital. Come in Double W One.'

The silence stretched into seconds that stretched into what seemed like hours. It was the longest wait of Tim's life.

TWENTY-TWO

Monet clambered heavily into her pilot's seat. Her shoulder blades burned as tears streamed down her face.

With a shaky hand and heavy arms, she scooped up the radio's handpiece as if it was a lump of lead from the floor.

'Elsie Creek Hospital. Come in, Elsie Creek Hospital. This is Double W One,' Monet said wearily over the radio.

'Elsie Creek Hospital. Go ahead, Monet,' replied Jenny.

'Um, can you…' Monet trembled as she wiped her mouth that seemed filled with cotton wool. She scrubbed at the tears and sweat that just kept falling. 'Tell Jasper he's got a baby girl. Both mother and baby are doing fine and we'll be wheels up in ten.'

'Oh, thank the stars,' said Jenny's relieved voice over the speakers. 'We'll be waiting. Have a safe flight.'

'Thanks. Over and out.' Monet would need it as she glanced at the setting sun that reflected off the floodwaters.

She climbed out of her seat to attend to her passengers. She strapped the dog in next to the little boy hugging his big teddy bear, wearing an even bigger smile. His tear-stained cheeks were a ruby red.

'I've got a baby sister.'

'You do, mate. You're a big brother now,' Monet said, ruffling his hair. He'd been a little champion.

Mother and baby sat in the seat behind him, where Monet checked over their seat belt. 'Keep breastfeeding the baby and she'll be fine.' The baby was beautiful with teeny tiny fingers and toes and the softest of skin. She was a miracle in Monet's eyes, which again welled with tears. A miracle.

'I will.' Even though Chrissie had tired eyes and sweaty hair, she had a calm glow to her while gazing at the suckling babe in her arms. They were a vision.

'Brendan, this is for you. All pilots and co-pilots get one.' Monet held out two of her precious candy canes. 'One for take-off and one for when we're landing, okay? The deal is, you have to suck on them only, no chewing. Can I trust you on that one?'

'Ah-huh. Ah-huh.' His head nodded like a wonky wheel about to roll away from a toy car, keeping his shiny eyes on the sweet treat.

'Good, because I don't share my candy canes with just anyone, you know.'

'I promise,' said the little lad, tearing at the candy wrapper.

'Get settled in guys, I'll just check out the plane.' Monet landed with a thud of her boots in the damp soil and staggered to the tail of the plane. She bent over with hands on her knees, taking deep lungs full of fresh air as sweat dripped from her nose.

It was quiet.

So quiet she heard the wings flap on a flock of blue-faced honeyeaters passing overhead. Their bellies reflected on the still waters that shimmered under the blends of gold and red spun by the setting sun.

Trying to shake away the trembles from the adrenalin in her hands, Monet inspected the undercarriage of her plane. She'd hit that ant mound hard and had landed badly. She needed to check for any hairline cracks because they were about to leave on the same crappy terrain.

Sure, she was wasting time, but she had to be sure for the sake of her precious cargo, and to calm her nerves.

'Thank you, Gertrude.' She patted her tough little red plane. She didn't care if people thought she was crazy talking to her plane. She'd spent a lot of time with Gertrude, who was a friend Monet could count on. 'Let's go back to town.'

She couldn't say home, because she was officially

homeless.

Homeless.

Some Christmas huh? Surely, she deserved better?

She certainly deserved better than losing her mind over some guy who was in love with someone else—like hell she was going to stick around for that wedding.

Why stick around at all? Stuck with a crappy reputation from an irreversible history. What about giving herself a proper Christmas present by rewriting her story somewhere else!

Her mother had escaped her horrible past, starting a new life in a new place and was blissfully happy. Didn't Monet deserve the same?

Monet looked back at the renovated farmhouse. Tucked away in her heart all her hidden hopes and memories rolled like melodies making her sway under the weight of nostalgia. She used to have a home, with her parents celebrating birthdays, and holidays, even that first visit from the tooth fairy. A home that had a family. Her family.

Her heart ached. Even though it wasn't the same house she stared at, everything reminded her of that god-awful Christmas Day twenty years ago.

Her dad gone. Her brother forever asleep. Her mother in shock. And she was that little girl left all alone with her dolly in a tiny house on a hill surrounded by water.

The tears blurred her vision. She wiped them away and put on her sunglasses as if mentally slamming her emotions into that little metal trunk kept locked tight and dropped to the bottom of a concrete bunker hidden under the floorboards of her bed. A hope chest that never saw the light of day.

She'd lost her belief in hope a long time ago. Hope only caused her heart to break in so many freaking layers, she'd come to fear anything resembling hope. And all those fears of hope failing used to give her nightmares.

Monet looked at the house surrounded by the encroaching floodwaters, overshadowed by a ginormous skyline. She followed it to where the water met the sky on the curving horizon to blend as one, as if gravity no longer existed.

Was it time to put those fears to rest?

Was it time to bring it all home?

Did she dare hope?

Determined, Monet climbed back into the plane and locked the door tight. As part of her routine, she again checked on her passengers and luggage. It was a routine she'd been using for over thirteen years, from her very first flight as a student pilot. A routine she was about to tap into along with all of that experience and most of all—the crazy side of her.

She was about to take-off without a runway!

Monet climbed into her lamb's wool covered seat, slipped on her harness, and strapped herself in tight. She flicked the dice and her traveller's good luck charm—twice.

Then she held her breath and punched the starter.

Like clockwork, the propeller wound over as she listened for the purr that allowed her to breathe again.

She peered back at her passengers, wearing their headphones. 'Do you guys have any music requests? Gertrude likes it.'

'Have you got any Christmas songs?' Asked the little boy, gripping tightly to his half-sucked candy cane in one hand, with the other holding onto his dog's collar.

'No. I don't do bells.'

'What about nursery rhymes?'

'Sorry. There's only adult music on board.'

'Grown-up stuff, huh?'

'Yep. Grown-ups are boring.' She felt a hundred years old, staring at what little land she had left with the rising water swallowing more every second that passed.

Monet taxied as far as she could on the shoaly paddock. She turned the plane to stand against the edge of the water, facing uphill. She didn't have long before this spot would turn into mud and bog them.

She'd flown off crumbling cliffs, but they were on smooth runways with a tailwind to help her. She'd landed on dirt tracks filled with bulldust and corrugations. She'd dodged cattle, kangaroos, donkeys, camels and buffalo, fighting whirly winds that crossed her path. She'd whizzed past flocks of circling kites through bushfires. She could do this.

She had to.

Monet struggled to get a fix on what the winds were

doing, but it was as if the entire world had paused to wait for her next move.

If there was ever a time to pray—this was it.

Throttle forward, the engine cranked up a notch as she held the plane steady, feeling its need to move. As the revs climbed, she released the brake and the little red plane rolled forward.

And she threw everything into it.

It raced towards the top of the hill and the plane's nose rose, then the wheels touched down. It bounced up. And down.

'Come on.' Through gritted teeth, Monet pulled back the yoke as the plane hit the top of the rise, gathering speed downhill. The strain made her arms tremble and her shoulders burn. 'Come on.'

This was it, they either hit the water and flipped or...

The wheels kissed the floodwaters, creating a small bow wave, scattering ripples across one huge pond.

Through the cockpit window, the reflection of the plane's straw broom got smaller and smaller as it climbed higher into the dusky sky.

Monet exhaled heavily. One by one she untangled her stiff and achy fingers from the controls, to flick the switch for the radio.

'Elsie Creek Tower. Elsie Creek Tower. This is Double W One. Over.'

'This is Elsie Creek Tower. How ya doin', kid?'

Monet wanted to smile. She wanted to sigh. She

wanted to say some smart-arsed comment, but she was tired. Dog tired. Rubbing her face to stay awake. 'We're in the air. ETA forty minutes. Have the ambulance on standby and prepare for a night landing. Oh, and a weather report would be handy. Over.'

'Night landing it is, kid. We've got light winds coming off the centre, that should give you a nice push,' relayed Mickey.

She could feel it and kept climbing to get clear of any downdrafts and turbulence. She wanted a smooth ride for her precious passengers.

'You're all clear on the radar for storm activity, so it's clear skies, kid. Aim straight and true and we'll see you soon. Over.'

'That you will. Over and out.' With her coordinates entered, she snatched up a candy cane for the sugar hit and flicked on her tunes, remembering to lower the volume for the baby on board.

She banked right, then straightened the plane to fly true north towards the tiny outback town of Elsie Creek.

Swallowing another layer of fear, she was determined for this family to have a happy ending. No one deserved to have a Christmas like she did as a kid. And Monet would not let history repeat itself—even though night landings scared the absolute living daylights out of her.

TWENTY-THREE

The sun had disappeared behind a purple haze, replaced by a blanket of clear bright stars, as Monet flew her tiny red plane over an incalculable, dark landmass.

No lights. No moving cars. Just a vast outback.

It was so peaceful in the air, she wanted to float up there forever.

'Is that the town?' called out Brendan with his little boots swinging high off the floor. Strapped into his seat, he held his teddy bear tight with one arm, the other was slung around his trusty canine companion, Bomber.

'Yes, it is.' The town of Elsie Creek shone like a metropolis and not some tiny outcrop in a remote region of the Northern Territory.

A place she used to call home.

Where was she going to sleep? Lucy's couch or Mickey's camp bed? She could always sleep in Gertrude. Not like she hadn't done that before, camping out at airstrips waiting for cargo or passengers to arrive.

But they were only temporary solutions.

She always had the Inn to stay at before she flew off on her next adventure. So why didn't she make the next trek an even bigger adventure?

It could be the search for a new home. A place she could reinvent herself, just like her mother did.

If she did leave, like her mother, would she be missed in this town? Or would she be forever remembered as the mad woman's kid infecting others with her madness? Sucking up for friends by keeping open the Inn, where she played the part as the madame sleeping with her many lovers?

But none of that mattered, not while she had a family to reunite.

'How are we doing back there, Mother?'

'We're good,' said Chrissie with a weary smile. 'I'm looking forward to a shower and food.'

'I hear you,' said Monet. Could she book in a shoulder massage with that too? 'Okay, Brendan, you know that second candy cane I gave you?'

'Oh, um...' He hid his little face behind the stuffed bear.

Monet grinned. 'It's a good thing I've got a secret stash, huh?' She reached into her glove compartment to discover the box was almost empty. 'What the heck, it's Christmas, right?' She tossed a couple back. 'Give one to your sister?'

'She's a baby, they've got no teeth,' said Brendan.

'I'll take it, I'm starving,' said Chrissie, unwrapping the candy cane.

'Okay, sit back and check those seat belts, everyone.' Monet wanted it to be as smooth as possible for the sensitivity of the suckling babe on board, who had slept the whole way.

'Elsie Creek Tower, this is Double W One. Over.'

'Elise Creek Tower here. Go ahead, kid.'

'We're making our descent now. The town is lit up like a...' She couldn't believe she was saying this, 'A Christmas tree.'

'Like that pearler you and Tim had with stars made out of beer cans. That's my kinda tree, kid.'

'Have you been cyberstalking me again, Mickey?' Refusing to think about Tim and their time together. That was the past.

She flew wide around the town. There were no house lights or street lights. Gone was that garish glow of flashing Christmas lights on the main street. The river spilled over the bridge and railway lines, where a simple flashing orange emergency light kept the *Road Closed* sign company.

What she'd give to see those garish red and green

lights highlighting the town's main street again.

'I can't see the runway. Or the airport. Only the cop shop. That roof looks good.' A new set of bright spotlights highlighted her artwork. Marcus had been busy—or was the town's top cop chewing up his generator fuel to show her the way to the airstrip?

'The cranky coppa is still spewing over his cop shop's new art display.'

'I'm sitting right here,' grumbled Marcus's voice over the speakers. It made her laugh.

'Listen, Monet, mate…'

Monet's ears pricked up; Mickey never used her name. Ever. But twice in one day—it made her bite down hard on her candy cane.

'You'll be landing on the back runway.'

'What? Why?'

'Well, kid, it's that new-fangled fire chief and all his bloody rules.'

'Oi.' Again, it was Marcus.

Monet shifted in her seat as a cold sweat broke into a fine sheen over her skin. Her grip on the yoke was getting slippery—which was never a good thing. 'I can't see the back airstrip. I don't know that strip to even do a hazard check cos it's dark. I was prepared to do the normal runway. I could. I really, really could. You know that smooth asphalted runway, not—'

'Claude.'

She froze with wide eyes, staring at the speakers. Was

she dreaming?

'You can do this.'

'Tim?' *Err, awkward!*

'Who else do you reckon it is? Now, I've gone to all this trouble to make you a present, so you need to come a little closer to see it.'

'Really?'

'Trust me, Claude. You'll like it. It's at the back runway, Mickey says, go around like you normally do and prepare for a final run. You'll see it then.'

Monet just stared at the speakers.

Somehow, the mere sound of his voice calmed the chaos swirling inside her.

'Are you still there?' Tim asked.

'I'm here. Flying over now… preparing for a landing. See you on the ground.'

'I'll be here, babe. Over and out.'

Babe?

She blinked at the speaker.

He called her *babe!*

Not a teasing, flippant babe, either. But the term of endearment kind. Loaded with a whole lot of tender mushiness that made her want to roll in a field of soft grasses, filled with wildflowers to stretch out under an outback winter's sun.

Err, reality check—she was flying blind in the dark!

Monet took a deep breath, re-gripped the plane's controls, and flew over nothing more than a blanket of darkness.

The hospital and the police station lights came up on her left as she did her best to get her bearings.

She now understood what Mickey wanted. It was all about routine. Whenever in a panic, she switched back to practising those flight patterns that were part of her routine.

They'd practised this, and it's what she always did. Fly over first, check for hazards, taking the time to look at the bigger picture.

She blinked, rubbing at her eyes as the main intersection of town came into view.

'Monet, are you seeing this?' Chrissie called out, wearing a wide smile. She pointed out the window to Brendan.

'What are they doing, Mummy?'

'I think they're having a Carols by Candlelight Concert.'

From her front row seat in the sky, Monet spotted the iconic pub with its lights that never went out. Over the road to the train station, lots of people had gathered on blankets to sit on the lawn. It was as if everyone was there, cradling a lit candle each, looking up to the sky.

It was a sea of soft flickering candlelight, just like those televised concerts they'd have in the city for carol singing.

Were the townspeople singing?

Today, she wouldn't mind it.

Turning off her music, she opened her side window,

but she was too high to hear them clearly. But a familiar scent filled her cockpit. Were they all using Kat's candles?

Monet flew from memory, around to the far end of the train stations' land, where the empty cattle yards could hold a thousand head or more. She just couldn't see them.

Swinging back over the railway line, the major highway and the sports field, home to the Dusty Dingoes in the dry season and the town's annual Rosella Festival. Again, all hidden under the cover of darkness.

But she knew they were there.

She'd flown over it all a billion times.

'Let's do this.' She gripped the controls tighter and spoke through her headset. 'This is Double W One, to Tower. I'm in position, ready for the final approach. If you're going to dazzle me, now is the time to do it. Over.' She hoped—yes, dammit—she *hoped* they knew what they were doing.

She saw nothing.

No lights.

No runway.

Nothing.

Then like magic, one after the other, flames burst to create individual lights that stretched in parallel lines ahead of her.

She had her runway under lights.

And right at the beginning of it was a massive X in flickering lights within a wonky row of words.

'What does that say?' called out Brendan.

'*Merry Xmas.*' Written in the dust by an entire sea of candles, with the biggest X she'd ever seen at the end of the runway.

She had her mark to aim for.

Monet wiped at the tears blurring her vision. The timing of her emotions sucked. She needed to find her spine and tap into all that craziness to finish this.

For the first time she swallowed her fear and swapped it for hope, bucket loads of hope, and gripped onto the yoke tightly. 'Brace yourselves, we're going in!'

TWENTY-FOUR

On the ground, Tim craned his neck back to watch the plane's lights move against a trillion complex constellations littering the sky. Monet's navigation lights and the buzz of the engine seemed so small compared to the cosmos.

He reached for the microphone, keeping his eye on his prize in the sky. 'Did you know, Claude, Gertrude's broomstick sparkles under the lights? I'll show you the pictures when you land.'

The worry and fear in her voice, he'd felt it.

But he also believed Monet had the skills to land anywhere. She could look at the curve of the land and spot the hazards in a matter of moments. But landing in the dark, on a dirt strip? That took loads of courage.

The fire trucks stood silently nearby. The ambulance was doing the same. All of the other spectators had been ordered back into town to wait.

And they had every single chunky candle they could muster. The flickering scented candles made the airstrip smell almost pretty—for dirt.

But they had to keep the new fire chief happy, and that meant using the old airstrip that was on the far end of the wilderness. It was nothing more than a patchy area they occasionally mowed, but it was free from any avgas tanks, planes, and other hazards.

Mickey's eyes lit up as his grin grew, watching his dunny rolls burn. They were being set alight by the firemen running along either side of the runway, playing pyromaniacs.

That left Tim, Mickey and Marcus to light up the Xmas sign he'd made for his angel in the sky. All under the careful eye of the fire chief in command of his crew, standing by their trucks with hoses ready to roll.

Tim had never truly fathomed the risk of night flying and what Monet did every time she got into her plane. In comparison, driving a car was child's play. Yet, Monet had the knack for making it seem so easy.

Now all he could do was watch helplessly as the floating broomstick in the sky came closer and closer. He was not going to lose her. Not now. Not like this.

The plane roared low above them. He crouched

down with Mickey as they scrambled for their seats on the golf buggy. Marcus kept his driver's seat, Mickey beside him, leaving room for Tim and Jasper in the back, both itching to run for the plane.

Wheels landed with a thud. They all heard it. Hell, he felt it rumble through his rib cage and he winced with worry.

Then the tumbling roll of the plane's wheels steadied.

'*Yahoo*, she's made it,' Mickey said, slapping that sweaty towel on his knee then twirling it in the air. 'She's bloody made it.' He patted Marcus in a half hug, knocking the beefy cop's hat.

'Steady on… Don't you two cowboys move,' Marcus warned Jasper and Tim, both men were eager to run for the plane's door. 'That propeller will make mincemeat out of you. We wait until the propeller's stopped.'

Jasper chewed what was left of his nails

Tim felt just as bad. 'Come on. Come on.'

The plane rolled to the far end of the runway, then turned. It's large row of spotlights bathed the darkness in hot white light and then they were switched off. The weighty silence was unbearable.

'Can a girl get a lift?' Monet asked over the speakers.

Tim smiled at the stars in pure shoulder-sagging relief.

'That's a go,' said Jax. The fire truck's lights lit up, kicking up the dust as it led the ambulance flashing its emergency lights. That left Marcus in the crowded golf buggy to follow in a very slow and rough ride.

'You could have used your fancy cop car for this bit, Marcus,' said Tim.

'Why? When I've commandeered this beast.' Rolling over every single dirt rut and weedy grass tuffet, it made for a very lumpy, slow ride.

The plane's door opened and out stepped Monet, holding the lead to a dog that bounded down the steps. She held a teddy bear on one hip and a little boy on the other. Her hair a mess, her eyes bright. And both Monet and the little boy sucked on the peppermint candy canes she rarely shared with anyone.

It was like a whip crack of light and he saw it as plain as day. It was messy. It was chaotic. It was completely unplanned, and in the middle of that storm was Monet. His Monet. He could picture her as a mother—the mother to their children. Having their own family, creating their own family traditions for generations to come—if she'd let him.

It was beautiful in all its messiness and disorder and she was so gorgeous, he couldn't stop staring at her. He'd been a fool to not see it any sooner.

The only problem was, how did he convince Monet?

Marcus nudged him on the shoulder. 'What are you waiting for? Go get your girl.'

'Yeah.' Tim wiped his mouth to check for drool.

He didn't need to be told twice. He'd been trying to catch her all day, and he wasn't going to stop now. He was never going to let her walk away from him, not until he told her what she meant to him. And Tim truly believed they were meant for each other.

Racing to the plane, he was met by the ambulance blocking his path. There, he helped them get the mother and newborn baby off the plane.

When he turned to find Monet… she was gone.

Are you kidding me!

TWENTY-FIVE

Under the torch's dim light, Monet kicked in the boards that made up the corridor wall leading to her bedroom in the Unofficial Elsie Creek Inn.

She climbed under the broken roof beams. Over the smaller branches, treading carefully through deep piles of leaves. The tree trunk lay solidly indented into the ground right through the middle of the house. The living room, spare room, kitchen, and bathrooms were demolished. Only her bedroom stood on the far corner of the house, with only three of it's four walls still standing, keeping her locked door in place.

With the bulk of the branches gone, they'd need some seriously heavy removal equipment to shift the trunk. But that was tomorrow's problem.

Right now, she needed to get inside her bedroom.

On her hands and knees, she forced her bedroom door open. Her bed lay under roofing tiles and plaster, with leaves everywhere. The entire room was on a lean. Most of the roof was gone, showcasing galaxies of twinkling stars as silent witnesses.

She had to do this now, so she scrambled along the floor on her hands and knees.

With the small tool lifted from her plane's tool kit, she pried back the floorboards.

The entire place creaked.

She froze, staring at the roof—what was left of it—until the place settled once again.

'Right, let's do this.' She gritted her teeth, wedging the tool in between the floorboards and yanked it back.

Creak! The wood cracked so loud in her ears as it split, she turned away in case of flying splinters.

Finally, she was able to pull the floorboard free. Then the next board and the next to create a hole big enough to reach into the gap beneath the house.

There, barely poking above the soil stood a circular concrete cap. She brushed away years of dirt built up around it to expose the edges. Twisting on the handle, the lid grated. Concrete against concrete, the noise rubbed against her spine. It was as bad as bells, which made her teeth ache.

Finally, after much strained effort, she had enough

room to push away the heavy concrete cover that landed with a thud. Her grandfather used to make it look so easy.

Monet aimed her torchlight down the hole to expose a deep and dry cavity. It was home to a tin trunk that lay at the bottom.

She reached into the concreted hole and dragged the trunk out by the handle. It was heavier than it looked, sapping all of her depleted energy to pull.

Determined, she re-positioned herself on the wooden floorboards that were leaning like a boat about to capsize. With both hands on the handle, her arms and shoulders burned and her legs trembled under the strain as she lugged the trunk up the sides. The squeal of metal scaping against the concreted sides of the hole grated on her nerves—it was worse than bells and rubbing concrete combined. It gave her the chills, as sweat trickled down the sides of her face.

On the concrete bunker's lip, the trunk's metallic base screeched against the floorboards as she inched it up and out of its grave. With her boot wedged against the edge, she dragged it up with all her might until it was free.

She collapsed on her back, exhausted, again staring at the stars.

'What the hell? Monet, are you—'

'Crazy?' She said to Tim, not surprised to see him crawling through the gap in the wall. 'Yep, I am completely and totally certifiable.' She juggled her set of keys, searching for the tiniest little brass key that sat next to

Gertrude's key.

There was never a key to lock the Inn. Only this box.

'What is that?' Tim asked, crouching next to her.

'Grandma Mary's hope chest.' She unlocked the trunk and lifted back the lid. They were soon forced back by the unseen cloud of gas that made their eyes water from the overpowering mothball odour.

'It's been a while since you opened this, eh?' Tim asked, fanning the air.

'I'd forgotten all about it until earlier today. I didn't think I'd get in here until I saw they'd cleared the tree. Did you have a hand in that?'

'Everyone did. We'll need a crane for the rest.'

We? 'I don't want them to burn the wood. I want something special made out of the timber. The tree deserves that much.

'I told them you'd say that.'

'Oh, and thank you for the Xmas in the dust thingy.'

'You could have said that with a bit more oomph.' Tim tugged on her hand making her look at him. 'Why did you run away like that?'

'Pfft, I didn't run. I just didn't feel like talking to people.'

He pointed at her. 'You were avoiding the awkward.'

She shrugged. Annoyingly, he was right. 'Can you shine your phone inside; my battery is nearly dead.'

'What's in here?' His phone lit up the contents filling the trunk.

'Memories,' she replied, fingering photo albums and assorted loose images. 'Hope…' Where her hope used to be buried so deeply it could never touch her soul. 'Did you think this was a treasure chest?'

He shrugged. 'How long has it been in there?'

'My grandparents built this when they built the house they never locked. They designed the bunker to keep their paper's dry in case of cyclones. Grandpa showed me this trunk after my dad's funeral. He called it our family's time capsule.'

Tim pulled out a tiny metal red plane from the side of the trunk. 'This isn't that plane I gave you?'

She nodded. Her throat too thick to swallow.

In the dim light she saw that boy, now a man, flick the propeller of the tiny plane and hand it back to her.

The small plane sat heavily in her hands, the toy that had started her lifelong obsession.

'For a minimalist, you really do keep everything, don't you?'

'Only the things that matter.' Even if it was a crummy little toy plane, it meant the world to her.

Tim reached out and smoothed down her hair. The simple gesture made another chunk of steel around her heart fall like the glass scattered around the house.

'Is that a wedding dress?' Tim asked, pointing inside the trunk.

Ever so carefully she lifted out a small fine white lace gown. 'It's Grandma Mary's bridal gown, made of spun silk and handmade French lace.'

'I heard from Esther, earlier today, that you're a proper blueblood who's related to the Queen. I'm surprised my mum didn't know; she'd be all over that.'

'I don't think so. Grandma Mary went rogue. She wanted to join the air force as a pilot, but being a female with a title, she wasn't allowed. So, she flew away to this place. Her father disowned her, forbidding her from ever using her title. The arranged marriage she had to some guy got cancelled too. Grandma Mary said she'd never been freer.'

'Because she was disowned?'

'They still gave Grandma Mary her dowry, which she used to build this place. Her mother would write regularly, and sent over this bridal gown as a gift,' she said, fingering the soft lace. 'Grandma Mary turned it into a christening gown for Mum. And me. And...' She picked up the photo that showed the portrait of her as a child, held by her parents. 'Grandma Mary had enough left to make a gown to bury my brother.'

She stared at the image.

She could face them now.

Her family.

After today, with what she'd been through, she'd found the courage to face her past, instead of trying to fly away from it.

It had also unearthed her dreams... and her hopes.

'I always wanted a family,' she whispered to the

photo. 'You know, the house, the dog, the car in the garage deal.'

'No way? With a white picket fence too?' He asked with his nose screwed up.

She mirrored his expression. 'Only if it guarded the veggie patch to keep the chooks out, I wouldn't waste my time painting it. But I'd have a bath.'

'Outdoors to watch the sunset?'

'Yeah, sipping nameless cocktails—'

'While making up names for clouds.'

She nodded. 'Silly, huh?'

'No, that's not silly at all.' He gave her a nudge that was both gentle and playful, sitting cross-legged beside her with the metal trunk in front of them. 'What's this?' He pulled out a small velvet box.

'I forgot that was in there.'

Tim opened it up, exposing a ring with a scattering of tiny diamonds that surrounded a small blue sapphire. It sparkled in the light of his phone.

It was small, but to Monet it was priceless.

'It was Grandma Mary's ring. She never took it off. Grandpa sold his prize horse for this ring.'

'A horse?'

'Yeah. Grandpa had this dream of training specialty horses that raced on sand. It's why he was out here, working as a fettler and training his racehorses. His life plan was all mapped out, until this angel flew in from the sky and his desire to marry her won out over everything else standing in their way. They were never apart.' She smiled softly at the ring as it sparkled in the box.

'You like this ring, don't you?'

'I do. It's not big or flashy, it meant something.' She then remembered, scowling at Tim who was supposed to be with the ex. 'Hey, what are you doing in here, anyway? I saw you with Shiny Sher—'

Tim leaned over and kissed her.

Her pulse spiked and lightning sparked behind her closed eyelids, twisting her veins into knots. It sizzled from her lips with a hot-white light of pleasure, all the way to her nerve endings.

She was so stunned she could only stare at him dumbfounded.

'Monet Mary Claudine Hill,' he said, plucking the ring from the box.

'Jeez, the Posh Prince remembered my name.'

'Will you marry me?'

'Are you crazy?'

'As crazy as you, and I wouldn't have it any other way.'

'You're not serious, are you? The man who plans everything?'

'Today I saw my future with you. All of it. It was crazy and messy, planned and unplanned, but it was us. This place,' he said, pointing to the stars through the hole in the roof, 'has always been a halfway house for people. It may have been a home for your grandparents, but it was just a place until we found our future homes.'

'Maybe for you as a guest, but for me it's not.'

'It is. Or you wouldn't have kept flying away from it, like you do.'

She gasped, hand to her throat. Was he right?

'Monet, I want you to come home with me where we'll make it a home just for our family. Not a halfway house, or a boarding house or an inn—but a home. I want to share both of my bathtubs with you, for the rest of my life, because I never want you to fly away and leave me behind again. In return, I promise you, right here and now…' Now on bended knee, he grabbed her filthy hand with broken nails from breaking into her own house, and held the ring out. 'I swear I will never ever leave you behind either. Not on Birthdays. Never on Christmas. And not on whatever-merry-day you want to call it.'

She gasped again, one hand covering her mouth while he still kept a grip on the other.

'You know we go together like lime loves tequila. Two separate ingredients that make the perfect cocktail.'

'You're making me thirsty.'

'I want to be with you as we create our own crazy mish-mash of cocktails and rules and traditions that will suit us and our family. What do you say?'

'Do you love me?'

'I'm on bended knee, proposing to you. What do you reckon?'

'I've never heard you say it.' But Monet had told Tim

she loved him all the time. He just never heard it the way she wanted him to.

'I love you, Claude.' He leaned in so close she could make out the individual lashes and the stunning kaleidoscope encased within his eyes, that whispered a warmth deep within her soul. 'I've always loved you. I just didn't know you wanted a family, until now, because you were always running away from it.'

'I won't.'

'What?'

'I mean, I will.'

He looked at her, unsure.

'Yes. I'll marry the Posh Prince, but no posh wedding.'

'You know, getting married will make this a contract for life.'

'You're lucky, I'm the kinda girl who isn't scared of paperwork.'

'My girl.' He slipped the ring on her finger. She threw her hands around his neck and shoulders and kissed him as the world leaned on its side in the middle of a destroyed inn.

Her heart and smile burst wide with joy and hope for the future. Her past was what it was and she let it go, because she had a future to plan with the man she'd always loved.

It was the dream she'd always hoped for.

'Do we go brag to everyone and join the street party?' Tim asked. 'Or do you want to hang in here and make out for a bit?'

'Mmm…' With the way that man kissed — 'We need the practise.'

'I'm all for practising.' Their lips met as their arms wrapped around each other. Beneath a trillion stars that peeked between the gaps of the broken roof, as the noise of the small outback town's street party filtered through, they celebrated their own party for two.

TWENTY-SIX

As the sun crept lazily over the distant horizon, dragging heat waves of humidity into the air, Monet and Tim carried the metal hope chest between them along the Elsie Creek airstrip.

Sun clouds shifted over waving silver leafed trees shading a soggy ground. The scents of fresh rain filled the air. The wet runway gave a glass-like reflection of the mighty red plane with its straw broom painted on the underbelly.

'Hello, Gertrude,' Monet said, patting the strong sturdy wings like a steed. She started her pre-flight checks as Tim loaded the trunk onto the plane.

'Hey, can we hang this toy up with your lucky dice and traveller's good luck charm in the cockpit?' Tim asked, holding out the tiny vintage red plane.

Monet compared the toy against the size of Gertrude behind it. 'Nah, it's a bit heavy for that, and the outback's heat might ruin the paintwork.'

'I'll find a special place for it at home, permanently,' he said, holding his hand over hers with the plane in the middle.

If he let go of her hand, she'd simply float away with his words.

Mickey, in his nifty golf buggy, came speeding over from the hangar.

'I see you got your cart back from Marcus?' Tim said.

'I did. Kid, she's good to go, fuelled and serviced,' Mickey said, seated behind the wheel. 'Hey, where did you two go last night? You missed the celebrations; it was a humdinger. I was expecting you to be dancing on the bar, kid.'

'We did our own celebrating,' answered Tim, nudging Monet. 'Go on, do the girlie thing.'

'Oh, right, the ring.' She winked at Tim and showed off the ring on her finger to Mickey.

'Blimey. Someone got all their Christmases at once. Congratulations, kid.' He clambered off his buggy and hugged the bride-to-be, then shook Tim's hand.

'We'll never forget the anniversary, that's for sure,' Tim said with his wide megawatt smile, sliding his arm around her shoulders.

'That's true.' They now had a brilliant reason to

celebrate Christmas creating their own traditions; and she wasn't afraid of it anymore. She also understood it—Christmas was about being with the ones you loved. It was also a celebration of hope.

A siren gave a short blast as the police patrol car approached them with Marcus behind the wheel.

'Are you here to commandeer my cart again, Sarge?' Mickey asked.

'That beast of yours is too much for me to handle this time of the day,' said Marcus, getting out of the slick highway pursuit car. He then nodded at the couple. 'I see Tim found you?'

'He did. Look.' Now she had a taste for it, she showed off her ring to Marcus.

'Congratulations,' Marcus said, shaking Tim's hand and kissing her cheek. 'I didn't think it'd be too long after Tim was ready to tear strips off Jax for getting in the way of making you that airstrip.'

'Yeah, my shot at signwriting by candlelight,' said Tim.

'Talking about signwriting,' Marcus said, opening the back door of his police car. 'I just went and had a quick look at the Inn to start on my preliminary reports, and found something interesting among the floorboards.' He pulled out a box from the backseat that was filled with different colours of spray paint.

Aw crap. She'd forgotten they were there.

'Any idea where they came from, Monet?' Marcus

narrowed his eyes at her.

Monet tried to step back, but Tim held her in place.

'Come on, Sarge, everyone knows Monet hasn't got an artistic bone in her body. She failed art in school,' Tim said, gently squeezing her shoulders. 'Anyone could have left that there, because everyone knows the Inn is never locked.'

'The lad's right,' butted in Mickey, cottoning on. 'It's gotta be from one of the guests. Everyone knows the Inn's never locked. Hey, is any of it glow in the dark paint? Could use some for the future.'

Marcus just kept staring at Monet.

She was trapped like a wallaby under a set of spotlights on the outback highway.

'Just like everyone knows that the Flynn brothers' movie marathon would never happen—but it did last night,' Marcus said.

'We missed that,' said Tim, nudging Monet. 'I'm not complaining. You?'

'Hell no.' She was in love. Totally, completely, hopelessly, head over heels. In. Love. With the Posh Prince, Timothy Kirby. And he loved her, just as she was, too.

'Gawd, they're in honeymoon mode already!' Mickey rolled his eyes as he started up his buggy.

'You're lucky I like you, Monet, and I owe you a lot.' Marcus said, sliding the box of spray cans into the boot of the police car. 'As for your artwork… I reckon it looks good under lights.'

'Is that why you put up those new spotlights?' Mickey asked.

Marcus gave a wry grin as he cleaned his sunglasses.

Clip-clop. Clip-clop. They all heard it echo across the tarmac, making them turn to look along the runway.

Sparkling tinsel wrapped around his wide horns and tail and the smudged words *Merry Xmas* were written in white chalk across his black coat. Cecil, the beefy water buffalo, stopped to rip up the grass on the edge of the runway.

'Oh, no you flamin' well don't, you menace,' grumbled Mickey, from behind the steering wheel of his nifty buggy. 'You get off my runway, I just swept that you overfed bag of bones.' The engine whined on his buggy as he sped away, waving his grey hand towel in the air like a stock whip, herding Cecil off his precious flight path.

'So, where are you two headed?' Marcus asked the couple, while Mickey whistled and yelled like an outdated stockman herding a mob of cleanskins. It was a lot of attention for one small pet buffalo.

'Home,' said Tim.

She mirrored his smile that shared a warmth expanding from inside her heart. *Home.* 'I'm still on holidays, with a contract to keep.' She didn't want to be too far from Tim, if she could help it.

'Stay in touch. Enjoy your holiday and I'll see you in the new year sometime.' Marcus tapped his police cap in a one-fingered salute and drove away.

Mickey, in his nifty cart, waved as he kept herding the water buffalo back towards town.

Tim and Monet faced the red plane glistening on the tarmac as the summer sun rose over the outback. 'How about it, Claude? We go home for good this time.' He held out his hand to her and said, 'Remember, I promised to take care of you.'

She felt it, holding his hand, she believed it. 'Let's just promise that we'll take care of each other.' And with a handful of hope, she was ready to fly away home.

THE END

Wait, there's more...

I have a gift for you!

Grab your FREE copy of

THE ELSIE CREEK
CYCLONE GUIDE

Only for Elsie Creek Readers!

Simply go to:

https://melarowe.com/elsie-creek-cyclone-kit/

Did you like the story?

If so, *your opinion* matters to me!

I'd love to read your review on
GOODREADS, BOOKBUB.

I'd also be doing my own *dance-in-the-dust* if you
shared the cover of this book on social media for me to see
how far this story has travelled!

Please add ***#Escape2HEA*** for me to find you.

With much gratitude,

mel

A . R O W E

Acknowledgements

Thank you

Thank you for reading this story of the fictitious town of *Elsie Creek.* She may not exist, yet there is a part of her found in the Northern Territory townships, roadhouses, dusty sports grounds, crocodile-crowded boat ramps, and even in the rural pubs sparsely scattered across northern Australia.

But here's a true story...

Ever since Cyclone Tracy annihilated our tropical city, Darwin, on Christmas Eve, 1974, our summers always start by preparing for the upcoming cyclone season. We update our cyclone plans, re-stock our cyclone kits, trees near powerlines get trimmed, and the councils run an annual cyclone clean-up.

After having lived through too-many cyclones, seeing the way nature bounces back is a miracle itself.

But it sure makes for a good story! Don't you think?

So, I'd like to thank those in our community who have helped with the cyclone preparations and clean-ups. They are the true champions of community spirit.

I'd also like to thank the many bush pilots I've known over the years. They certainly gave me a spectacular bird's-eye view of their office in the sky, while dodging assorted wildlife on various outback airstrips. You guys are the untold legends of the Territory and a necessity to our lifestyle—especially during the wet season.

Thank you to the amazing Handbrake for not disowning me

whenever I burrow down into a new story. I'd also like to thank the rest of my family who have never read a word I've written, so again, I'm putting this right here in case they do dare to indulge.

Thank you to my online writer friends who've helped me so much when I live in a world where finding decent wi-fi is like discovering gold. Thank you to my critique partners and the Fabulous First Readers team; I am truly blessed to have you join me on my writing journey.

Thank you to the quirky, colourful, and exceptionally extraordinary people I've met while working and living throughout northern Australia. The experience has been—and continues to be—priceless.

Thank you, because I can, because I did, and because I continue to do so...

Until next time,

A. ROWE
australian bestselling author

ABOUT THE AUTHOR

Australian bestselling author, Mel A ROWE, creates escapes for today's busy women to enjoy from the comfort of their home.

Delivered with a dash of drama, witty humour and quirky family units, Mel is known for reinventing romantic versions of home, taking her common characters on uncommon journeys that lead from boardrooms to billabongs as they try to find their own HAPPILY EVER AFTER.

Living in Northern Australia, Mel enjoys random outback road trips, fumbling with her camera, annoying her family with her bad singing, and making new friends in the middle of nowhere—except for water buffalos. She's been chased by a few.

Feel free to contact Mel, as her word journey continues, at...

MelAROWE.com

www.ingramcontent.com/pod-product-compliance
Lightning Source LLC
Chambersburg PA
CBHW032002130726
47903CB00012B/493